"Sex doesn't have to mean marriage. But sex between you and me would never be casual."

"You figure if we make love, then, you'll be immune to me? Sex as a glorified flu shot?"

"I'm not that naive, Morgan."

"All we do is fight!"

"That's because we're two loners used to having our own way who've been thrown into a kind of intimacy we both abhor."

"So this sex we're talking about—it's not going to be casual, but it's not going to last and it's not going to be intimate. Forgive me if I'm a little confused."

Riley shoved himself to his feet. "You think I've got it all figured out?" he blazed.

"I hate this," she shouted back. "Is it intimacy you abhor or is it me?"

"Don't be coy," he snarled. "You infuriate me, you arouse me, and in thr[ee] my world upside down. [...] you, Morgan Cassidy."

Although born in England, **Sandra Field** has lived most of her life in Canada; she says the silence and emptiness of the north speaks to her particularly. While she enjoys travelling, and passing on her sense of a new place, she often chooses to write about the city which is now her home. Sandra says, 'I write out of my experience; I have learned that love, with its joys and its pains, is all-important. I hope this knowledge enriches my writing, and touches a chord in you, the reader.'

Recent titles by the same author:

SEDUCING NELL

UP CLOSE
AND PERSONAL!

BY
SANDRA FIELD

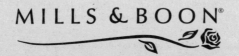
MILLS & BOON®

First published in Great Britain 1997
Harlequin Mills & Boon Limited,
Eton House, 18-24 Paradise Road, Richmond, Surrey TW9 1SR

© Sandra Field 1997

ISBN 0 263 80606 5

Set in Times Roman 10½ on 11¼ pt.
01-9802-54357 C1

Printed and bound in Great Britain
by Mackays of Chatham PLC, Chatham

CHAPTER ONE

THIS is what happiness is all about, thought Morgan.

She scraped the last bit of yogurt from its small plastic container, knowing that after two or three days, when her freezer packs had melted, she'd be reduced to powdered milk and dried food. She let the yogurt slide down her throat—raspberry yogurt, her favorite—and gazed at her surroundings.

Her campsite was perched on a ledge overlooking a dried-up streambed edged with squawbush and the delicate tassels of rice grass. The late afternoon sun made the limestone cliffs glow a warm orange, as though they were lit from within. From a scattered clump of pinyon pines a scrub jay squawked unmusically, and behind her water dripped monotonously from the cliff face; otherwise the silence was complete.

She was only four miles from the highway, but she could have been a hundred miles from it. She was also, of course, thousands of miles from home…briefly her green eyes clouded and her soft mouth thinned. She didn't want to think about home. Home or school or Chip or Sally. She only wanted to be alone. Alone in the desert for two whole weeks. Or longer, if she chose to be.

You've got until Christmas, Morgan Cassidy, she told herself, watching an errant wind ripple through the grasses. Two months to get your life back together. And where better to do that than in this enchanted place in the Utah desert, a place you've been coming to for the last four years?

Carefully she tucked the plastic container into a garbage bag and put her spoon aside to wash later, when she got supper. Then she stood up, stretching to her full five-feet-ten, wriggling her toes inside her sturdy hiking boots. One last trip back to the car, and she could settle in for the night. For the night and for the next two weeks.

Heaven. Absolute heaven.

Also a long overdue heaven, she thought wryly. Things had started to fall apart last autumn, and here it was October, a full thirteen months later.

She checked that she had her car keys, put her empty pack on her back and clipped her canteen to her belt before climbing down from the ledge to the streambed. It was cool in the shade. Maybe she should bring back that extra sleeping bag. While she'd never camped here in the fall, she knew the temperature could drop dramatically at night, and she hated being cold.

One more reason that every summer she came here to the desert.

Surefooted, she wove her way down the gully, then turned into a narrow side canyon with its steep upward slope and its smoothly eroded walls. Emerging onto slickrock, she tramped on, eyeing the pines and junipers along the way as affectionately as though they were old friends. A chipmunk scurried across her path; high in the cloudless sky, a red-tailed hawk scanned the desert floor. To her left the great mesas and monoliths of the state park cut into the horizon.

With an unconscious sigh of repletion Morgan stood still for a minute, the sun catching in her tumbled mass of red curls, inadequately pulled back with a leather thong. Was Boston, where she lived and taught school, home? Or was this place home? Home to her spirit in a way the city could never be?

Yet she had never once thought of moving permanently to Utah. It was as though she needed the contrast, she decided thoughtfully, all the demands of a city so completely different from the solitude of the desert. Two extremes. Wondering if this were true, she began the slow descent to the riverbed that followed the highway, automatically placing each step with care. A sprained ankle was the last thing she needed.

Then suddenly she stopped dead, all her senses alert. What was that sound she'd heard? An animal in pain? Standing stock-still, her ears straining, she waited to hear it again.

Nothing. Only the utter, enfolding silence of the desert.

She hadn't imagined the sound. She was sure she hadn't.

Once she had heard the scream of a jackrabbit as it was seized by a coyote; this sound had been nothing like that. More like an animal caught in a trap.

Morgan looked around, taking her time. To her left was a wind-scoured basin of limestone, punctuated here and there by spikes of yucca, a vista totally open to her eye: nothing could be hiding there. To her right there were boulders, a cliff face, and the dark slits of side canyons. She retraced her steps, peering around the boulders, ducking behind a venerable, twisted pine and a lacy elder tree. Still nothing.

The wind rustled through the elder leaves. Shrugging her shoulders, she clambered back to the path. While she didn't like to think of an animal suffering, the creature, whatever it was, was long gone. Beyond whatever help she might have offered. Trying to put the incident out of her mind, she tackled the next slope.

Ten minutes later Morgan heard the swish of cars from the highway. Ever since she'd found her campsite four years ago, she'd been hiding her car in a grove of cottonwoods and tamarisks, and not once had she run into trouble that way. Confidently she left the riverbed and headed for the road, enjoying the stretch in her leg muscles, already looking forward to getting back to camp. The feathery branches of the tamarisks brushed her sleeves.

"Stand still! We've got you covered."

With a gasp of shock Morgan froze in her tracks, and for a crazy moment wondered if she'd wandered into the set of a Wild West movie; quite a few had been filmed in the deserts of Utah. Hands up, she thought foolishly, and watched as two men thrashed their way out of the bushes. The first one had a rifle slung over his arm. When he saw her, his jaw dropped, as did the barrel of the gun.

Hunters, Morgan thought with a surge of relief.

"Who the hell are you?" the second man squawked.

He was shorter than his companion, greasy brown hair poking from the brim of his Stetson, a ragged mustache adorning a face that was blessed with neither character nor intelligence. In a flash Morgan made a decision: she didn't want this rough-looking pair knowing she was camping anywhere in the vicinity. Even though her heart was beating erratically under her dark green shirt, she said coolly, "I've been hiking. Who are you?"

The first man, whose eyes were a very pale blue— predatory eyes, thought Morgan with an inward shiver— said after the smallest of pauses, "FBI, ma'am." He pulled a wallet from the pocket of his jeans, flipped it open and shut it all in one quick movement. "You see anyone while you were out hiking?"

"FBI?" she repeated blankly.

"We got a tipoff that an escaped convict's in the area. Not a fella to fool with—long record of violence."

She remembered the sound that had set her searching among the rocks and felt her blood run cold. As she opened her mouth to tell them about it, the second man yelped, "But, Howard—"

"Shut up, Dez, I'll do the talking. You see anything, ma'am?"

Dez, obediently, kept quiet. Morgan said steadily, "No. Not another soul. What he's done, this convict?"

"Armed robbery. Shot a policeman. You sure, ma'am?"

She wasn't sure at all. "I didn't even see any hunters," she said.

Howard scratched his chin, his eyes narrow with suspicion. "If you're hiking, where's your vehicle?"

"I hid it in the cottonwoods," she answered casually.

Howard gestured with the gun. "We'll just check it out, if you don't mind, ma'am."

Morgan did mind. But she'd never had any dealings with the FBI, and Howard didn't look like the kind of man to brook any of her objections. Glad that the highway was so close, comforted to hear the whine of passing cars, she skirted the tamarisks and led the way through the smooth trunks of the cottonwood trees; and with every step she took, she wondered why she had lied to them, and if they'd notice that her backpack was empty. Hikers didn't head out into the desert with empty packs.

Her little rented car was cleverly hidden from the road. She said redundantly, "There it is."

"Unlock it, would you?"

She did as he'd asked, and watched in silence as Howard gave it the once-over. Her car was, very obviously, empty. He said expressionlessly, fastening those pale eyes on her face, "You going back to Sorel?"

"Yes, that's right."

"Then I'd suggest you do that right away, ma'am. And I wouldn't go hiking anywhere in this area. Not if you value living."

I don't like you, Morgan thought. And I'm not at all sure you're FBI, no matter what you say. She undid her pack, and, endeavoring to look as though she was hoisting a weight from her back, put it on the back seat. Howard passed her the keys. His fingernails were dirty. "Thank you," she said politely. "And good luck with your search."

"Don't you worry," Dez said with gusto, "we'll get the sonofa—"

"I told you to shut up," Howard said venomously.

Her nerves twitching with fear, Morgan slammed her door, started the car and carefully drove over the uneven ground toward the highway. A red half-ton truck was parked on the shoulder. There were no other vehicles in sight. She turned right as though she were heading into Sorel, slipped into second gear and didn't look back.

She didn't care if she ever saw Howard again.

Sorel was ten miles down the road, a tourist town that catered to visitors to the state park. Morgan drove for two of those miles, her shoulders tense, her fingers gripping the wheel. Then she pulled over, keeping an eye in her rearview mirror.

Why hadn't she told them the truth? That she had heard something—or someone—out there on the trail?

Did FBI officials drive rusty old trucks and carry rifles? Could they look quite as dim-witted and brutish as Dez? And why hadn't she insisted on looking more closely at the card in Howard's wallet?

Because she'd been afraid it hadn't been legitimate. That's why.

More questions marched through her head. Had the sound she'd heard back there in the desert come from human lips? *Was* there a convict? If not, then why did Howard and Dez so obviously want her out of the way? Howard of the cold, predatory gaze...

In Boston, Morgan's fellow teachers had never known her to hold back from a tight situation; chewing on her lip, she checked her mirror and eased the car off the road, following the tracks of an all-terrain vehicle until she was hidden from sight among the cottonwoods that edged the dry riverbed. Swiftly she shoved the extra sleeping bag in her pack, along with as many water containers as she could carry. She got out of the car and checked that it was indeed hidden from the road. Then, feeling like a character in a spy movie, she tweaked half a dozen hairs from her head and painstakingly positioned them in the car doors, the trunk and the hood. Locking the car, she pocketed her keys.

She was nuts. Who did she think she was, a female version of James Bond? The sensible thing to do was go to Sorel, check into a motel for the night and find out if a convict was indeed on the loose anywhere in the area.

But Morgan had traveled a very long way to camp under the stars tonight; besides, her campsite wasn't easy to find—that was one of its charms—and neither Howard nor Dez looked the type to go blundering around in the desert at night.

If I'm to be strictly honest with myself, she thought, keeping to the trees as she headed back the way she'd come, I don't think an animal made that sound I heard. I think a man did. And I'm putting all my money on the simple fact that I don't trust Howard as far as I could throw him. I'd be willing to bet it's the first time Dez heard the story about the convict; which is why Howard kept telling him to shut his mouth.

If they're FBI, then I'm a member of the CIA.

So who was the unknown man?

That's what I'm going to find out, Morgan told herself stoutly. But first I'd better check out Howard and Dez. Just in case they have headed into the desert.

Forty minutes later Morgan caught her first glimpse of the red truck; it was parked in exactly the same place as it had been when she'd left. She slid her pack off her back, stashed it against the trunk of a cottonwood, and edged toward the truck, acutely careful to make not the smallest of noises. And then she heard the mumble of voices from behind the truck.

Crouched low, taking advantage of every patch of grass along the way, Morgan crept around some ragged clumps of rabbitbrush until she could distinguish words. Then she sank down to stillness. ''I don't see why we ain't out lookin' for him,'' Dez was saying fretfully.

With heavy sarcasm Howard said, ''And what're we going to do when we find him, Dez?''

''Finish him off,'' Dez said with considerable relish.

''Oh, sure, we'll just pump him full of bullets…don't you remember what my idea was? My idea was to make it look like a hunting accident. An accidental shooting— they happen every year. But no one's going to think it's an accident if the guy's got a dozen bullets in him. Or if his head's bashed against a rock. I know you're not high on brains, but for Pete's sake use the few you got.''

There was a pause while Dez, presumably, endeavored to do so. ''So what're we gonna do?'' he said finally.

''We're going to sit tight. We'll patrol the highway just in case he gets to it, and other than that we'll wait until the buzzards start circling. That way we'll know he's a goner.''

As Morgan gave an involuntary shiver, Dez said, ''If you'd aimed higher, we wouldn't—''

''Belt it, Dez,'' Howard said, his voice so ugly that Dez stopped talking and Morgan shrank lower behind the bushes. ''I shot him in the leg, right?'' Howard went on. ''That way he can't walk—we hardly even need to patrol the highway, there's no way he could reach it. And we moved his car so it's not so easy to see, because we don't want any state troopers wondering about this guy before he's done for. So we haven't got a worry in the world. Blood loss and dehydration'll finish him off, and there we've got it—one more poor sucker who got in the way of a stray bullet.'' His voice smug, he finished, ''All we gotta do is wait. Then head for Salt Lake City. Lawrence'll pay us, and pay us good. Easy money, Dez. The kind I like.''

''You think that broad'll tell 'em about us in Sorel?''

''Nope.'' For the first time there was another note in Howard's voice. ''She was quite a looker, that one.''

''Her hair was kind of a mess.''

''It wasn't her hair I was looking at,'' Howard leered. ''C'mon, let's get something to eat.''

As the truck doors opened and slammed shut, Morgan seized her chance to back away. Her brain was whirling. She'd never had any dealings with the FBI, but she was more than ever convinced that Howard and Dez were anything but federal investigators. Why would the FBI try to make a convict's death look like a hunting accident? And if there really was a convict, they'd be out there searching for him, wouldn't they? Along with as many of the local police as they could muster.

So who *was* their unknown victim? And why had they shot him and left him to die?

Whoever he was, he was out there in the desert with a bullet in his leg. If—her stomach gave a horrible lurch—he was still alive. Why, oh why, hadn't she searched more diligently when she'd heard that sound?

She snaked her way back to her pack, shouldered it and headed as quickly as she could for the riverbed. This was her chance, while Howard and Dez were eating, to get back on the trail to her campsite. A trail that would take her past the place where she'd heard a man cry out in pain.

Morgan walked fast, no longer caring how much noise she made. The sun was sinking in the sky; although she had a flashlight, she'd just as soon not have to travel in the dark. Feeling her boots grip the slickrock, she climbed higher, and all the while her ears were alert to every tiny noise. Then she reached the tumbled boulders where she'd looked around for what she'd thought was a wounded animal.

Standing still, she listened, sifting the cool air for the slightest of clues, her eyes darting every which way. Nothing. Only the silence of ageless rocks and a vast sky, and the softest of whispers from the elder tree. She said in a carrying voice, "I know you're around here somewhere. Just tell me where you are, and I'll get you to a doctor. I'm quite safe, you can trust me."

Then she waited. Still nothing.

"Please," she said. "I heard Howard talking about you, I don't think you're a convict. You can trust me—please."

Slyly the wind brushed her cheek, mocking her. Even the birds were quiet, she thought in faint desperation. She walked to the basin, searching for any signs of footsteps, for scrapes on the rock. For bloodstains, she thought with a frisson of her spine. Not to her surprise, she found nothing. Reluctantly she turned to face the boulders and cliffs. The side canyons were pitch black slashes in the rock.

Morgan had camped alone in the desert for the last seven years, had taken courses on desert survival and considered herself not easily frightened. But right now she was frightened. Afraid of what she might find? A man now dead whom she could have saved had she searched more thoroughly a couple of hours ago? Or was she more afraid of finding nothing?

Trying to stay calm, she unclipped her pack, leaned it against a rock and climbed to the first of those black clefts, all the while keeping her eyes open for rattle-snakes or scorpions and her ears open for the slightest of sounds. She took out her flashlight and shone it on the canyon walls, absently admiring the sinuous curves carved by centuries of erosion. She followed the canyon for about twenty feet until it narrowed in a way that made further passage impossible. Backing up, she crossed to the next one. It, too, petered out, about fifty feet in.

The third fissure was wider, its floor made up of small stones that crunched under Morgan's boots. As she shone her flashlight along the walls, her heart gave a great thump in her chest. A palm print was etched on the smooth rock. Etched in dried blood.

At age six Morgan had decided she'd be a medical doctor in the far north when she grew up. At age seven, when her father had cut his thumb on the carving knife, she'd discovered that the sight of blood made her feel faint, dizzy and sick to her stomach, and had changed her plans: she'd be a jet pilot instead. Unfortunately, she'd never really outgrown that childish reaction to the sight of blood.

She stopped and said in as normal a tone as she could muster, ''You can trust me. I'm not in cahoots with the two men who shot you...I'm here to help you, please believe me.''

Her voice echoed eerily in the limestone chasm. With a superstitious shudder Morgan felt as though the rock itself was listening to her, waiting with bated breath for her to leave so it could resume its ageless, patient waiting in this land so rife with death. Taking a deep breath, she trained the flashlight on the walls again and took a dozen more steps. There was another smear on the rock, this one lower down, as if the man had stumbled and almost fallen. There was also a long gouge in the stones on the canyon floor, and a scattering of drops of blood.

Dried blood. The man had passed this way a while ago.

He either wasn't an expert on the desert or else he was desperate, Morgan decided, picking up her pace.

She herself never ventured into these narrow canyons with their steep walls because of the danger of flash floods. However, she'd been following the forecast ever since she'd crossed the border into Utah, and the past couple of days had been bone dry all over the state; so there was no immediate threat. She walked faster, only wanting this very nasty adventure to be over.

Fogetting to be cautious, she swung the beam of light ahead of her, seeing the walls narrow and the rock rise a good ten feet higher, her eyes scanning for the telltale signs of blood. Then some sixth sense flashed her a warning; she whirled to the movement she'd caught from the corner of her eye.

An arm clamped itself around her waist and a hand was jammed over her mouth. Something hard dug into her ribs. A gun, she thought wildly. He *is* a convict. Oh, God, what've I done?

CHAPTER TWO

MORGAN'S back had been hauled against the man's body and she felt as though she was smothering. She tried to bite his palm, but he was pressing too hard. Wriggling frantically, she tore at his arm with her one free hand and dug in her nails, and might as well have been trying to dislodge a steel girder. Going on instinct, Morgan raised her booted heel and kicked out hard.

She connected with flesh and bone, heard a shocking, brute sound of raw agony, and felt his grip drop from her mouth and her waist. She staggered free and turned to face him, noticing with a small part of her brain that her flashlight had fallen to the ground and was illuminating a small circle of colorful, scrabbled stones.

In the dim light she watched her assailant thrust his hand into his mouth to bite back any more sounds. His face was contorted with pain. Her gaze fell lower until she saw the rough, bloodstained bandage wrapped around his thigh under his jeans. His right thigh. The leg she had kicked.

Leaning hard against the opposite wall of the canyon, she said faintly, "I'm *sorry*...I'm so sorry. But you frightened me."

His body was hunched over. He was wearing jeans, hiking boots and a light shirt. A haversack rested at his feet. Morgan stepped forward, picked up the flashlight and turned it off, from some obscure notion that the man's struggle to contain his pain was a private struggle, and not for her eyes. Gradually her vision adjusted to the gloom. Adjusted enough so that it was horribly clear to her what a huge effort it took for him to straighten,

17

shoving his back inch by inch upward along the canyon wall.

He braced himself against the rock, resting his weight on his good leg. His breathing was harsh, his eyes sunken black sockets in his skull, and several achingly long seconds passed before he was able to speak. He rasped, ''Well, you've got me. Aren't you going to signal the others to finish me off?''

He was a big man, several inches taller than she, and even under circumstances as horrible as these he was maintaining a kind of aloof dignity. This was not, Morgan thought with a dry mouth, a man who would beg for mercy. Rather he would fight to the very last, using every weapon at his command.

Keeping her distance, she said, ''Which prison did you escape from?''

He gave an ugly laugh. ''Don't play games, lady. Do what you've got to do and let's get it over with.''

''I know you're an escaped convict.''

Sheer rage flashed across his features in a way that made her blood scurry in her veins. ''Cut it out!'' he snarled.

Morgan's intuition had stood her in good stead in many a nasty situation in school, and with a tightening of her chest she decided to trust it once more. ''All right,'' she said. ''They told me you were an escaped convict, but I don't think you are. So I'm here to help you—I'm nothing to do with the two men who shot you.''

''Then how do you know about them?'' he grated, that same rage flickering just below the surface.

She took a step away from him, sensing that it would take very little for him to launch himself at her. Speaking as calmly as she could, she said, ''I was hiking here earlier in the day and heard you, but I couldn't see anything—I thought you were an animal of some kind. Then when I went back to the highway I met these two men who said they were FBI looking for an escaped convict. Their names were Howard and Dez. They told me I should head for Sorel and stay there. I didn't believe them altogether, so I eavesdropped and heard that they'd shot you and were going to wait for—'' her voice faltered in spite of herself ''—thirst and blood loss to finish you off. So it would look like a hunting accident. Once you were dead, they'd get paid by someone called Lawrence.'' In a rush she finished, ''That's why I came back looking for you.''

''Florence Nightingale,'' he sneered.

It had been a very long two hours and Morgan's temper tended to be as unruly as her hair. She said trenchantly, ''I'm trusting those guys weren't on the up-and-up, that you're not a convict. Despite the way you're behaving. That's what I'm doing. So now you've got to trust me, that I'm not in league with them. Why don't we cut out the small talk, agree to get along, and figure out how the heck we're going to get you to a doctor?''

''Where are the two men?''

''Parked by the road a couple of miles back.''

''I'm not going anywhere near that highway tonight,'' he announced. ''I don't have a clue what's going on, but I'm sure as hell not going to set myself up for them to try again.''

''You can't stay here! If I can find you, so can they.''

She heard the edge of panic in her voice and added, ''Dez isn't smart enough to fight his way out of a paper bag. But Howard's a killer. And you'd better trust me on that, too.''

''I need a drink,'' the man said tightly. ''I finished all my water three hours ago.''

Morgan unclipped her canteen and with the feeling that she was making a momentous decision, crossed the narrow canyon floor and passed it to him, her level gaze meeting his.

She was well within range should he have chosen to strike out at her and immobilize her; she knew that and so did he. He said softly, "You've got guts, lady, I'll give you that," and unscrewed the canteen, raising it to his lips and taking a long drink.

The muscles in his throat moved smoothly. Morgan averted her gaze. "I've never liked being considered a lady," she said. "Calls to mind crinolines and tea parties and dainty little parasols. My name's Morgan. Morgan Cassidy."

He passed her back the canteen, his fingers brushing hers. "Riley Hanrahan."

"My campsite's half an hour from here," she said crisply. "It's well hidden, and I've got a good first-aid kit. Do you think you can make it?"

"I don't think I've got much choice," he said.

She bent and picked up his haversack, putting it on her own back. "Let's go, then. One of the hardest parts will be getting out of here, it's so narrow."

Riley pushed himself away from the wall. "If you go just ahead of me, then I can lean on you."

She gave him a quick grin. "You'd better give thanks for all the nights I sweated at weight lifting in the gym last winter."

"Yeah…you're beautiful when you smile, you know that?"

Morgan's jaw dropped much as Howard's had when they'd first met among the tamarisks. She bit back the answer on the tip of her tongue, the almost overriding temptation to respond, "You're the sexiest man I've come across in my entire twenty-nine years and you're not my type at all." Instead she said tartly, "It'll be my muscles that'll get us out of here, not my pretty face."

"I didn't say pretty. I said beautiful. Move it, Morgan Cassidy."

Morgan glared at him. She didn't like men who towered over her. She liked being able to look a man straight in the eye. Right, her mother Frances had once said, irritably for Frances, who was the most even-tempered of women. You want the man in your life to be like an old flannel shirt, one size fits all and no surprises.

This was not the time to be thinking about men or her mother. Morgan took a deep breath and turned her back on Riley.

They shuffled their way back down the canyon, Riley's hand heavy on Morgan's shoulder. He couldn't quite mask the tiny grunts he made with each movement of his injured leg; Morgan was perspiring by the time they reached the exit to the slickrock. She whispered, "You stay here. I'll scout around and make sure no one's out there, and I'll hide my pack so I can come back for it later."

His hand tightened cruelly on her nape. Then, deliberately, he released her. Knowing that by so doing he was trusting her to return, a huge admission on his part, she gave him an edgy nod. Soft-footed, she walked out of the canyon.

Darkness had fallen. A three-quarter moon was rising over the distant buttes and with a small lessening of tension Morgan realized she wouldn't have to turn on her flashlight; she was reluctant to do so even though she was almost sure Howard and Dez were snug in their truck at the edge of the highway. She walked back to her pack, checked it for scorpions and lugged it to the canyon where Riley was waiting. He said, "You know what I hate the most here? The fact that I'm putting you at risk, too."

Although he had spoken evenly, she didn't need any of her training in psychology to discern the frustration and rage that infused his words. Bending, her spine a long curve, she filled the canteen from one of the water bottles, passed him a nut bar and watched him devour it. "Neither Howard nor Dez struck me as the type to go gamboling around the desert at night," she said lightly. "Our greatest risk is that you'll trip and fall flat on your face and I won't be able to pick you up. Weight lifting or no weight lifting."

"Two-ten, stripped," he said.

"One thirty-four," she replied, her imagination presenting her with an instant and very graphic image of him stripped. What was wrong with her? She'd never been one to be turned on by a sexy man. And if this wasn't the time to be thinking about her mother, it was certainly no time to have sex on the brain, either.

He said, the first touch of humor warming his voice, "I'll do my best to remain vertical, Morgan Cassidy."

"You do that, Riley Hanrahan."

She tucked her pack well back into the canyon, then said, "Let's go. We'll walk for ten minutes and rest for ten. And no macho arguments."

"I'm feeling about as unmacho as it's possible for a guy to feel. Let me walk on your left side, that way I can use you as a crutch."

A crutch was a very asexual way to regard a woman, thought Morgan. If this undoubtedly sexy man saw her as a piece of wood, so much the better.

It took nearly two hours for Morgan and Riley to reach her campsite, two hours that would long remain in her memory as one of the most excruciating ordeals of her life. If she'd had any thoughts of behaving like a piece of wood, they were soon banished. Riley didn't say much after they set out. He didn't need to. She could see all too clearly the cost to him of every movement, his gathering exhaustion, his stubborn courage and refusal to give in. Someone had once told her the best way to get to know a man was to take him to bed. She was discovering another way, she thought crazily, shouldering most of his weight as they inched with agonizing slowness down the slickrock. Haul a man across the desert with a bullet in his leg.

Was the bullet in his leg? She didn't even want to think about that. Get to the campsite first, Morgan, she told herself. One thing at a time.

They reached level ground, and with an unconscious sigh of relief she felt Riley straighten and thereby relieve her aching muscles. He said harshly, swiping at his forehead, "God, I hate this—I don't even know you, and here I am falling all over you as if I've been on a three-day drunk."

"Just be glad I'm five-feet-ten and not five-feet-two."

"I like tall women," he said, and gave her an unsteady grin.

He was swaying on his feet. She said, suddenly flooded with an anger whose cause was a mystery to her, "Good for you. I don't like tall men. Do you want to take a rest?"

"Nope. If I sit down now, I'll never get up. What've you got against tall men, Morgan?"

His voice, even hoarse with exhaustion, went right through her, so deep and resonant was it. "Riley," she said furiously, "tomorrow morning we can have a nice little discussion about all our preferences in the opposite sex. But not right now. Right now we've got the worst part ahead of us—another side canyon. It's the reason my campsite's so well-hidden. So let's not fool around with chitchat, okay?"

"The worst part?" he repeated. "I didn't think it could get any worse. Give me a drink, will you? And make it straight whiskey."

"Now that *would* be a really stupid thing to do."

"Are you by any chance a school teacher?" Riley said quizzically. "You bring to mind old Miss Cartwright, who could see right through your math text to the comic book you'd hidden behind it. Eyes like gimlets and a tongue like a ripsaw."

"Oh!" Morgan seethed. "You're impossible. Come *on*!"

With a lopsided grin he said, "Keep your sense of humor, sweetheart."

"I am not anyone's sweetheart," she said, each word falling like a small stone.

"Too crabby, I expect," he said cheerfully.

Why did he have such a knack for knocking her completely off balance, in a way that had nothing to do with his arm around her shoulder? Well, maybe nothing. With exaggerated patience she asked, "Are you or are you not coming with me?"

"Guess so," he said. "My choices, as I believe I pointed out earlier, are minimal."

"Thanks a lot," she said sarcastically, and felt the heft of his arm fall back around her neck.

As they angled their way through the side canyon, Riley said nothing more. But Morgan was achingly aware of his harsh, indrawn breathing, of his bitten-off groan as he struck a rock with his right foot. She was aware of much more than that. Her whole body was steeped in him: the jut of his hipbone, the ridged arch of his rib cage, the dig of his fingers into her shoulder when the pain got too much for him. His shirt was soaked in sweat; but underlying that was something much more earthy, the scent of one man's maleness. She felt as though he was becoming ingrained in her, in a way that made her profoundly uneasy.

Keep your cool, Morgan, she adjured herself. We'll soon be there.

Ten minutes later they emerged into the streambed. "Another hundred yards," she said.

Riley gave an indecipherable grunt, and hobbled along beside her across the tumbled stones until they reached the ledge. She said, hearing her voice quiver with stress, "There's my tent."

He had been leaning on her more and more heavily the last few minutes; her shoulders and wrists were aching from supporting him, and her knees felt like jelly. He said in a hoarse whisper, "You mean I get to sit down and stay down?"

Morgan drew on the last reserves of her strength and half-levered, half-lugged him up the slope to the ledge. "Yes," she said, and felt tears of sheer relief prick at her eyes. "Hold on while I unzip the flap."

He said with considerable force, for the shape he was in, "I'd rather sleep outside."

"With the scorpions and rattlesnakes? I don't think so. Okay, down you go."

It was a mark of Riley's exhaustion that he didn't argue. Morgan did her best to lower him gently. But all her muscles were trembling with strain, and she heard him gasp as he landed hard on her sleeping bag. She climbed in after him, zipped the flap and flicked on her flashlight. In the small circle of light she had her first good look at him.

Hair the color of the burnished leather straps on her backpack, eyes the blue of a desert sky. A crooked nose, a cleft chin, well-defined cheekbones that to her over-wrought imagination seemed to make a statement about the man. His cheekbones and his jawline, she thought. All equally uncompromising. She undid her canteen, took a long swig and passed it to him.

He drank deeply. Putting the canteen down beside him, he leaned back on one elbow. "Safe," he said.

"Yes. This ledge is invisible from above. I've camped

here for four years so I've checked that out.'' Her voice, to her horror, was shaking.

Shoving himself upright and taking one of her hands in his, Riley said roughly, ''Thanks, Morgan—I'd be dead meat if it wasn't for you.''

She winced at his choice of words. The glow from the flashlight lit the lines of strain around her mouth, the faint blue shadows, like bruises, under her eyes. Eyes which looked green and depthless, set under brows as imperious as the wings of a hawk. Her tangled red curls glowed like an aureole, framing a straight nose, softly curved lips and a very decided chin. Riley opened his mouth, as though he were about to say something else, then closed it again.

Morgan scarcely noticed. It was odd, she thought vaguely, that after supporting his body for the better part of two hours, the warmth of his callused palm should make her want to cry.

Avoiding his gaze, she said, ''Are you hungry? And I'd better heat some water so we can bathe your leg.''

''Look at me, Morgan.''

Unwillingly she raised her eyes. ''You saved my life,'' Riley said, the startling blue of his irises boring into her. ''I'll never forget what you did the last couple of hours…you're the bravest woman I've ever met. And no, I'm not the slightest bit hungry, although I suppose I should be.''

She snatched her hand back. ''I'm not brave, I just couldn't have lived with myself if I'd done anything different,'' she muttered. ''I'll light the stove and heat some water.''

As though his words had taken the last of his strength, Riley lay back on her sleeping bag and closed his eyes. She unlaced his boots and eased them off his feet, and made a pillow out of the thickest of her sweaters. As she put it under his head, he gave her a quick smile of thanks, and she could see the tension slowly ease from his long body. He murmured, "The bullet passed right through. Slather my leg with antibiotic, that's all you need to do."

Right, she thought ironically, and went outside to light her camp stove. The moon had climbed higher, casting velvety shadows below the cliffs; the stars spangled the desert sky, brilliant in a way they never were in Boston. At this precise moment she would have given her extremely expensive hiking boots to be all by herself in the little bathroom of her Boston apartment turning on the taps for a hot shower.

Instead Morgan boiled a small pot of water and carried it back to the tent. Riley was asleep, his cheek curved into her sweater, his long lashes brushing his tanned skin. You're not my type, she thought with unexpected fierceness. I like my men well-groomed, pleasant-featured and as even-tempered as my parents. You're much too rough and tough for me, Riley Hanrahan.

So what? a little voice whispered in her head. You're not out here looking for a man. So what does it matter what Riley looks like? Tomorrow you'll go into Sorel and get help, and then you'll never have to see him again.

Tomorrow wouldn't be soon enough.

Not liking the tenor of her thoughts, Morgan undid her first-aid kit and laid out its contents. Then she looked down at Riley. She couldn't very well cut his jeans away from his leg; he'd have to wear them again when they left here. Every nerve screaming a protest, she reached for his waistband.

As she slid the metal button from its buttonhole, his eyes flew open. She said flatly, "I've got to take your jeans off."

"Hell," he said. But he undid the zipper and lifted his body so she could ease them down his hips. The fabric was stained rust around the wound in his leg; very carefully she pulled his jeans down over his ankles. His legs were long and strongly muscled. Her eyes skittering away from the dark hair on his calves, she untied the rough bandage around his thigh and discovered that it was stuck to the wound. She soaked the cloth in water and with infinite gentleness pulled it away. Making an inward plea that she not disgrace herself, she forced herself to look at the bullet wound.

Her stomach swooped and the color drained from her cheeks. Come on, Morgan, she told herself frantically, there's no one else here. You've got to do this.

"You okay?" Riley rapped.

"No," she said in a thin voice. "I've stopped fights in the corridors, I've taken knives away from kids high on drugs, and I can make the toughest guy in the entire school back down. But the sight of blood makes me dizzy."

"I knew you were a teacher," he mumbled. "Dump some peroxide on it and wrap it in a bandage, that's all you need to do."

She said fractiously, "That's like telling someone who's afraid of heights that all they've got to do is climb Mount Everest."

"Get it over with, Morgan. Because it's going to hurt and if I don't get some sleep soon I won't be answerable for the consequences."

She folded a towel and put it under his thigh. "I washed my hands outside," she said weakly, undoing a sterile pad and dipping it in the water. As lightly as she could, she put it over the wound. He flinched. Her teeth clenched, trying to think of anything but what she was doing, Morgan did her best to clean the jagged, bruised flesh with water and then with antibiotic ointment. It was, fortunately, only a flesh wound; it could have been a lot worse.

Riley didn't make a sound. But from the corner of her eye she could see the beads of sweat on his forehead, and the bunched fists at his sides. She put on new pads and looped a bandage around his leg, clipping the ends.

"I've finished," she quavered.

Very slowly he loosened his fists. "Come here," he said.

"I—"

"Morgan, do as you're told. Lie down beside me. Now."

Morgan disliked taking orders, a trait that sometimes got her in trouble with the authorities at school. But there was something in Riley's voice that made arguing impossible. She lay down on his good side. He put an arm around her, pulled her close and stroked her hair back from her forehead with a gentleness that made the last of her defences crumble. Burying her face in his shoulder, she started to cry.

She wept from fear and weakness and horror; then she sobbed into his shirt, "This is so s-silly, there's nothing to cry about, I shouldn't even—"

"Shut up," he said economically. "You outwitted two armed thugs, got assaulted in a pitch black canyon, hauled two hundred pounds of dead weight halfway around the desert, and then had to cope with what sounds like a genuine phobia. You can cry all you like. You've earned it."

Chip had always made fun of her fear of blood. One last sob tore at Morgan's throat. "I—I suppose you're right," she gulped.

"Of course I am. Are you always this hard on yourself?"

He'd touched a nerve. She sat up and said much more vigorously, "My character need not concern you. Now or ever. Go to sleep, Riley!"

"Only one sleeping bag. It's going to be a tight fit."

She swiped at her wet cheeks with the sleeve of her shirt. "I'm going back to the canyon to get the pack I left there. There's another bag in it."

Riley grabbed her by the wrist, his fingers like handcuffs. "You're not going back out there!"

"I've got to! Those side canyons are just where Howard and Dez would look for you, we can't risk them finding my pack. Anyway, it's too cold for me to do without a sleeping bag, and my water supply's in that pack, too."

He said savagely, "I hate this! I'm about as useless as a day-old kitten. I don't want you going anywhere near those guys, Morgan, they shot me in cold blood."

"Why?" she blurted.

Although the word had escaped without her volition, Morgan had no desire to retract it. As she waited for his reply, she realized how crucial it was. Did she, deep down, still believe he might be a convict? That Howard and Dez, however unorthodox, were really federal agents?

"You think I don't want the answer to that question?" he snarled. "The trouble is, I haven't got a clue."

"They wanted it to look like a hunting accident. Why would they do that?"

"The guy with the gun saw me hiking across the rocks, raised the gun and shot me. Deliberately. It was no accident. That's the one thing I'm sure of in this whole mess." He gave a humorless bark of laughter. "Hell, maybe he'd just bought himself a new rifle and wanted to try out, and I happened along as the first available target. That makes as much sense as anything else I've come up with."

"But he left you there." Morgan shuddered. "There's got to be a reason."

"If I figure it out, I promise you'll be the first one to know."

"Are you very rich?" she said naively. "Or powerful? A politician maybe?"

"No, Morgan, I'm not. Do you think I haven't been racking my brains ever since it happened? And come up with zilch? Leave it alone, for Pete's sake! The fact remains there are two gun-happy animals out there, which is why I want you right here where I can keep an eye on you. God knows what they'd do to you if they caught you."

"They won't catch me," she said shortly. "I have to get the sleeping bag and the water, Riley, there's no choice. So you've got to trust me...I'm no more anxious to come face-to-face with Howard than I was to look after that dreadful hole in your leg."

He fell back onto the sleeping bag, his swearword making her blink. Then he added violently, "Take the goddamned flashlight, at least."

"All right," Morgan said with a meekness that probably surprised her more than him. "If for any reason you have to go outside, wear your boots...snakes and scorpions travel at night."

He gaped at her. "You mean that quite apart from that creep Howard, I've also got to worry about rattlesnakes getting you? Just don't tell me you camp in the desert for pleasure!"

"The number of deaths from rattlesnakes is extremely small," Morgan retorted. "And I love camping in the desert."

"You're out of your mind."

She put her palm flat on his chest. "Oh, stop it! You don't have to worry about me, will you get that through your thick head? I'm a totally competent twenty-nine-year-old woman who's been coming to the desert for the last seven years. Your problem is that you hate being dependent on me."

He winced. "You see too much, Morgan Cassidy."

His eyes narrowed. "When you're angry, it's as though your hair's smoldering, and your eyes are like green flames. Get moving, will you? The sooner you go, the sooner you'll be back."

She scowled at him, this man who spoke pure poetry one moment and the next was ordering her around as if she were ten years old, not twenty-nine. "I forgot to give you an antibiotic tablet," she said, opened her kit and passed him two of the pills for good measure. "I'll be gone for three-quarters of an hour. Is there anything else you need before I go?"

For a moment his eyes lingered on the softness of her mouth. "If I asked for what I really need, I have the feeling you'd slap my face." Frown lines indented his forehead. "Plus I'd know *I* was clean out of my mind."

He wants to kiss me, Morgan thought blankly. That's what he means. And at the same time he hates himself for wanting to. Her cheeks stained with color as bright as blood, she found her spare flashlight in one of the side pockets of the tent and put it beside him. "The best thing you can do is rest," she said severely.

"Yes, Miss Cartwright."

"You'd better remember what I said about the toughest guy in the school," she threatened, and reached over for the other flashlight, her shirt drawn taut over her breasts.

"Are you married? Or otherwise taken?"

His question had come out of the blue. Tense as a wild horse about to bolt, Morgan gasped, "No. Are you?"

"No." With genuine urgency Riley added, "Take care, Morgan—please."

Something in his voice made her pull her scattered wits together and respond with equal seriousness, "I will, I promise. Sleep well."

She unzipped the tent and got out, closing the flap behind her. Moving with instinctive care, she slid down the ledge.

CHAPTER THREE

THIRTY-FIVE minutes later Morgan's footsteps were crunching along the gully. The journey had gone without mishap; there had been no sign of Howard or of rattlesnakes, and the walk had both calmed her nerves and relaxed her body. She'd be able to sleep now, she thought confidently, and lithely mounted the ledge.

The tent was unzipped, the flap hanging open.

Her heart gave an ungainly leap in her breast. She hoisted the pack off her back and knelt down, shining her flashlight inside.

Riley was gone.

The sleeping bag was disarranged, his shirt flung to one side. His jeans and boots were gone, too.

Howard. Howard and Dez had found him and taken him away.

With a whimper of horror Morgan backed out of the tent and looked around, her eyes huge as she searched the deep shadows at the base of the cliffs for a man's dead body. Because Howard would finish Riley off this time, she knew that in her bones.

The scrape of a booted heel against rock ripped along her nerve endings. She whirled, her body hunched defensively, and in the moonlight saw a tall man, naked to the waist, wearing jeans and boots, limp around the corner of the ledge. Riley.

He was alone.

Gracelessly she sat down on the ledge and dropped her head to her knees. Fainting's getting to be a habit with you, Morgan Cassidy, she thought dimly, and with a detached part of her brain heard Riley shuffle closer.

''Morgan! What's wrong?''

Her voice box felt paralyzed and she was trembling all over. Mutely she shook her head, wishing him a thousand miles away.

''For God's sake—are you hurt? Morgan, say something…I can't get down to your level, if I do I'll never make it back up.'' His voice roughened. ''*Morgan…*''

Very slowly she raised her head. The ledge stayed where it was, firmly beneath her, and the moon didn't plummet from the sky. Wishing she'd stop shaking, she got to her feet, wavering a little. He reached out for her, clasping her by the shoulders. ''Tell me what's wrong!''

She said tonelessly, ''When I got back I saw that the tent was open and you were gone. I thought Howard had taken you.'' A shudder ripped through her frame. ''That you were d-dead.''

Somehow she was in his arms, being held hard to his bare chest, her cheek nestled against his collarbone, his heartbeat thudding against her breast. Safe, she thought. I feel safe.

''I drank too much water,'' he said. ''Nature was calling. That's why I was gone.''

She was still trembling, like the leaves of the cottonwood trees in a summer wind. ''Next time,'' she muttered, ''leave me a note.''

''A five-page letter,'' he promised solemnly. ''I figured I'd be back before you were.''

''It didn't take as long as I thought it would.''

''If it's any help, I sweated blood every minute you were gone.''

''Good thing I wasn't there to see it,'' she said with a shaky laugh and heard his answering chuckle.

''No sign of Howard or Dez?'' he asked.

''Nope.''

It had been an extraordinarily long day and Morgan was light-headed with tiredness. As confidingly as a puppy, she rubbed her cheek against the dark hair on Riley's chest. "You feel good," she said naively. "I don't usually act like a hysterical female."

Riley dropped his cheek to her hair, then she felt his mouth brush her forehead in the lightest of caresses. The shock ran through her body as though she'd touched an electric fence. She pulled back, babbling, "I don't usually collapse on the nearest man in a crisis, either."

"I doubt very much that you do," he said dryly. "Let me tell you something else. I'm in the habit of heading in the opposite direction when a woman collapses on me. Or has hysterics anywhere in my vicinity."

But he hadn't turned away from her. He'd been available in a way that had touched her to the core. Morgan announced, "I need to go to bed and sleep the whole night through. That's what I need. As soon as possible."

Ignoring her, Riley said levelly, "Seems like a lot of rules are being broken between you and me. What is it, four hours since I jumped you? Feels like forever."

She was almost sure he meant none of this as a compliment to her charms, and she was in no shape to talk about rules, broken or otherwise. "You go first," she said.

The moonlight made a gash of his mouth and deep pits of his eyes. Very deliberately he pulled at the leather thong that bound her hair back and fumbled with the knot until it loosened. After shoving the strip of leather into his pocket, he buried his hands in her hair, tugging it around her face in a wild cloud. "There," he said. "I've been wanting to do that for what feels like forever, too."

Morgan no longer felt safe. Not the slightest bit safe. She was trembling again. This time it had nothing to do with the fear of finding Riley's dead body and everything to do with the live man: with the sweep of his palm down her cheek, the pull of his fingers at her scalp, the blatant exposure of a need of his that she could in no way explain. Or explain away.

This was the man she was going to sleep with. A man who was, in most ways, a complete stranger to her. While she didn't think he was in any physical shape to fall on her in the night, she'd also had proof of his prodigious powers of endurance. "Riley—" she croaked.

"You're scared of me," he said blankly.

Her innate truthfulness getting the better of her, Morgan nodded miserably. "I'm not used to sharing my sleeping space. And I always come here alone."

"Morgan, do you honestly think I'd repay the courage and kindness you've shown me by trying to seduce you?"

"Please don't be angry! I—I'm so tired I don't know what I think. But you're—"

He said tautly, "I've been insulted a few times in my life but that takes the cake."

Her temper flared. "Oh, does it? Let me tell you something, Riley Hanrahan. You're five inches taller than me and seventy pounds heavier, and in that first canyon I had a taste of how strong you are. Don't you dare pretend that physically we're equals!"

"All men are not rapists."

"I never said they were and what the *heck* are we doing standing here yelling at each other when all we both want to do is go to sleep?"

He ran his fingers through his hair. "Good question. Got an answer?"

She loved it when laughter warmed his voice: a voice that reminded her of the amber depths of the very best brandy. "Not tonight," she said.

"Me, either." He gave her a crooked grin. "Give me an arm to get back in the tent, will you, Morgan? And then I swear I won't touch you again."

She hesitated. "I really hurt your feelings, didn't I?"

His grin vanished as quickly as it had appeared. "You could say that. Which is another rule gone out the window. I don't let women close enough to me that my feelings are ever in any danger. The tent, Morgan. Now."

Why don't you?

For a moment she thought she'd spoken the words out loud. Horrified at herself, Morgan crouched down so he could lean on her as he levered himself through the flap, and felt every contact between his body and hers ricochet through her. "I'll join you in a few minutes," she mumbled, and turned to get her pack. She wouldn't spend one more second thinking about Riley Hanrahan's behavior, she swore, stashing the water bottles on a shelf in the rock where she knew they'd be safe. Then she shook out the extra sleeping bag, very thankful that she'd brought it along. It would be even better if she had a three-person tent rather than one that slept two.

For several minutes she gazed up at the stars, hoping their cold, ancient light would restore to her a sense of proportion. Riley was just a man. That's all. A man who'd been thrown into her company at a time when her reserves were nil and her craving for solitude absolute. No wonder she wasn't handling the whole situation with much grace.

She'd even lost her appetite, she thought with a touch of amusement, remembering that in all the excitement she'd forgotten about supper. She who loved to eat.

A good night's sleep would do wonders for her. Tomorrow she'd get help, then she could resume her holiday undisturbed.

She'd forget about him as easily as she'd forgotten about supper.

Morgan eased herself into the tent backward, dropped the sleeping bag and shook the dirt from her boots, lining them up in the corner. She zipped the flap shut. Riley had aligned his sleeping bag against the far wall; as she glanced over at him, she saw that he was watching her, one arm angled behind his neck. Dark hair nestled in his armpit. The hair on his head was thick, cut short like the pelt of an animal.

She straightened out the extra bag and rummaged in her pack for a T-shirt. "Close your eyes," she said. Quickly she hauled her shirt over her head and pulled on the T-shirt. She never wore a bra when she was camping; the T-shirt made this all too obvious. Yanking off her bush pants, she slid her long legs into the sleeping bag and grabbed her jacket to make a pillow. The space of about five inches separated her pillow from Riley's. She turned her back. "Good night," she said in a strangled voice.

"Sleep well, Morgan."

Sure, she thought, and within five minutes was both deeply asleep and completely oblivious to the fact that for quite a long time Riley lay awake watching her.

Daylight woke Morgan. That and the piercing squawks of the scrub jays, those sky-blue marauders whom she admired for their skillful array of survival tactics. For a moment she frowned, because the sleeping bag pulled up to her chin was not her own purple one, but a dull brown. Then memory surged back and she looked over to her right.

Riley was still asleep, his body turned toward her, one arm closing the gap between the two sleeping bags. His hand lay on the dull brown fabric. His fingers were crisscrossed with small white scars, and his palms were those of a man who works outdoors, not at a desk. Beautiful hands, Morgan thought unwillingly. Lean, strong and capable.

He suddenly heaved himself sideways, muttering something under his breath. Her head reared up.

Alarmed, she saw that his cheeks were flushed and his hairline damp with sweat; he was plucking at the soft goose down. Disentangling herself from her sleeping bag, Morgan rested her palm on his forehead. His skin was burningly hot.

All her movements swift and decisive, Morgan got dressed, then went outside, completing her own toilet as quickly as she could. Taking a facecloth and one of her precious water bottles, she went back to the tent.

When she put the cool wet cloth on Riley's face, he pulled away. "No, sister," he muttered. "No…"

So he had a sister, she thought, adding this to her small stock of knowledge about him and persisting in her ministrations. Perhaps five minutes later his eyes flickered open. They looked at her without recognition. He said clearly, "Tell Anna I'll be late for dinner."

Quickly, Morgan raised a glass to his lips. "You must drink," she urged. "And I have a pill for you to take."

She slipped an antibiotic pill onto his tongue and held the glass to his lips. As obediently as a child he drank the water. "You'll tell Anna, won't you?" he repeated.

"Yes," Morgan said calmly, "I'll tell her."

His eyes closed. She should have woken him in the night and insisted he take a pill then, she chided herself, more frightened now than she'd been when she'd walked into Howard and Dez in the midst of the tamarisks. Because Riley had no idea who she was.

And who was Anna?

You can worry about that later, Morgan Cassidy. Right now you've got to bring his fever down.

She read the relevant section in her first-aid book, and in some trepidation checked the bullet wound, finding it, to her huge relief, clean and less swollen than it had been last night. She laid wet cloths on Riley's chest and forehead, spoke to him softly when he was most agitated, and tried very hard not to mind when over and over again he repeated that one name, Anna.

Anna was nothing to her. Any more than Riley was.

By midafternoon, when he seemed worse rather than better, Morgan was thoroughly worried. He should have a doctor, not her own less than expert attentions. But how could she leave him here alone while she hiked and drove all the way to Sorel?

What if she met up with Howard again?

He was so restless that she'd long ago undone his sleeping bag to give him more freedom of movement; she was sure it was only his injured leg that kept him from heaving himself across the tent. For the umpteenth time she wrung out her cloth and reached over to bathe his chest.

In a raw voice he cried out, "She's busy...you mustn't bother her, it's not important!" Then, as the cool cloth touched his flesh, he struck out with his fist.

Because Morgan was bending over him, he hit her full across the breast, driving the air from her lungs with bruising force. Her shocked cry of pain sounded very loud within the confines of the tent.

Riley's eyes sprang open, dazed blue eyes that focused on her with difficulty. But they were focusing. Seeing her, Morgan. Not Anna or his sister or the unknown woman whose busyness had caused him such distress. Morgan exclaimed, "Riley—"

He said thickly, "I hit you..."

"You didn't mean to, it's okay."

"I heard you cry out." He shook his head like a stunned animal fighting its way back to reality, and pushed himself up on one elbow. "Morgan, I'm sorry—"

She seized her opportunity. "Riley, I've got to get a doctor. I'm so worried about you, I don't—"

"No!" He fell back, his chest heaving. "No doctor."

"The police, then," she said desperately. "Howard tried to *murder* you, we've got to get help."

"No doctor, no police."

In a small voice she said, "Are you in trouble with the law? On the run from someone?"

"No…I swear I'm not." Visibly she watched him gather his strength. "The only way you're heading…for that highway is when I'm with you in good enough…shape that I can flatten Howard if we run into him. You got that?"

"You've been delirious all day," she protested frantically. "I'm afraid of you getting worse."

"All *day*? What time is it?"

"It's nearly four. It was yesterday I found you."

She could see him trying to process this. "Aspirin," he whispered. "That'll take the fever down."

She found the bottle of aspirin in her kit and passed him two. "Four," he mumbled, and swallowed them one by one. Then he reached out for her. "Promise you won't go, Morgan. I couldn't bear for anything to happen to you because of me."

His scarred fingers were clamped around her wrist. Oddly she felt as though in the last few minutes their roles had shifted, as though he was the one now in command. "I won't leave unless you get a lot worse," she said.

"I won't…I won't get worse." He struggled for breath. "Keep talking to me, will you? So I won't…drift off again."

By sheer willpower this man's going to force himself back to rationality, she thought incredulously. Because he hit me by mistake. Because he doesn't want me running into danger.

Nothing remotely like this had ever happened to her before.

Striving to keep her voice even and reassuring,

Morgan began to talk. She described dawn in the desert with its glitter of dew on the grasses; the silvery-turquoise berries of the juniper, the lizard's deep blue tail, the scarlet flowers of the prickly pear cactus; the rainbows that could arch from horizon to horizon; the fall of light and shadow on the curves of limestone and the curves of snakes. And all the while Riley's gaze was fastened on the vivid expressions that crossed her face and on her graceful gestures as she spoke of the land she loved.

She was telling him about the time she came face-to-face with a mule deer when suddenly she became aware of a change in his breathing. He had fallen asleep. A natural sleep, she realized with an immense surge of relief. The fever had broken.

His hand was still curled around her wrist.

As though she were a lifeline, she thought humbly. The rope the drowning man grasps with all his strength because he knows it will save him.

She sat very still, aware that her knees were cramped and that she was thirsty, yet reluctant to move and break the spell. It was a spell, she thought honestly. A different reality than any she had ever known.

All her life her parents' marriage had been her model: their even, steady relationship, courteous, kind and reliable when all around her her friends' parents were fighting, separating, divorcing. No raised voices, no ugly arguments, and always the certainty of true affection. So, ever since she was a teenager, Morgan had been searching for the man who would give her that same calm sanctuary from the worries of the world. Searching and failing to find.

For a long while she'd thought Chip was the perfect man.

Until thirteen months ago.

Riley sure wasn't. There was nothing calm and reasonable about Riley Hanrahan. He was a man who gave orders right and left, astounded her by his formidable willpower, and annoyed her by laughing at her when she most wanted to be serious.

So why was she crouching here with pains shooting up her thighs? Because she didn't want to detach his fingers from her wrist? Because all too clearly he had needed her help in battling down delirium and fever?

Chip had never needed her. Nor had she needed him. At the time she'd thought this was entirely commendable, and had rather looked down her nose at those of her friends entangled in what she had viewed as less subtle and much messier relationships. She had, she remembered, pictured herself as a smooth, glassy lake, her friends like frenzied ocean waves battering themselves against immovable cliffs.

What a superior bitch I must have been, she thought now.

Although she still had no idea how to achieve a marriage like her parents'. Was that one of the things she'd come here to sort out?

That, and her teaching career, and burnout, and Chip, and Sally's illness. That's all.

With a rueful smile Morgan stretched out her legs. It was past time she had something to eat. She hadn't come to the desert in order to starve herself.

Very gently she freed her wrist. Riley muttered, "Morgan?"

He hadn't said Anna; he'd said Morgan. "It's all right, I'm just going to get myself something to eat. Are you hungry?"

He shook his head and briefly his eyes flickered open. "You tied your hair back."

"It's a nuisance loose, it gets in the way."

"Gotta change that," he said in a slurred voice, and drifted off to sleep again.

Oh no, you don't, she thought rebelliously. The way I wear my hair is nothing to do with you. I'll wear a wig if I want to. A blond one.

Giggling a little at the thought of her face framed by artificial yellow curls, Morgan went to get herself something to eat.

CHAPTER FOUR

AT DUSK Morgan was propped against a rock reading by the light of two brass candle lanterns, her fleece jacket wrapped around her shoulders. A good meal and four hours of solitude had done wonders for her spirits; she felt equal to anything. So when she heard Riley moving around in the tent, she called out, ''Need any help?''

''No, thanks.''

There was something repressive in his voice; or was her imagination working overtime? A few moments later she watched him lever himself out of the tent. She scrambled to her feet and hurried over to offer him an arm. He said impatiently, ''I can manage, Morgan. I've got to get back on my own two feet.''

She stepped back. ''It was only yesterday you got shot in the leg, Riley. Go easy on yourself.''

''That's the opposite of what I plan to do.'' He limped past her and disappeared around the ledge.

He hadn't once looked her in the eye.

She went back to her book, although it was difficult to concentrate, and when she heard him coming back, asked, ''There's stew or spaghetti, which would you prefer?''

''Spaghetti. Please.''

He sat down carefully on the rock nearest her, rubbing at his good leg. ''Have you eaten?''

She nodded, busying herself with her stove. ''How are you feeling?''

''As if I've got the great-grandfather of all hangovers.''

She glanced up. The candles cast wavering shadows

over his face; he was badly in need of a shave, his hair was rumpled, and his eye sockets bruised. "You look awful," she said, and grinned at him. "Almost as bad as Dez."

"We've got to get out of here," he said restlessly. "Maybe tomorrow."

He hadn't smiled back, and he was talking to her as though she were a stranger, not the woman who had saved his life. She flared, "We've got two choices. Tomorrow I can go for help and bring back a couple of paramedics with a stretcher plus a whole squad of policemen. Or else you and I can walk to the highway. Which means we wait for another three days. Minimum."

"You're not going anywhere near the highway on your own."

"Then we'd better be prepared to put up with each other for three more days."

"I heal fast," he snapped. "Where's your car?"

She stared at the spaghetti sauce as it sizzled around the edge of the pan and said politely, "Is your sister expecting you?"

He frowned at her. "What are you talking about? I don't have a sister."

"You mentioned your sister while you were feverish. Quite a lot. Her name's Anna, isn't it?" Morgan asked, and waited to hear if Anna was indeed his sister, and not some other woman. A woman who must have meant a great deal to him. A woman who, for some reason, she was prepared to dislike.

His breath hissed between his teeth. "I don't have a sister!" Before Morgan could gather her courage to ask who Anna was, he went on in a clipped voice, "And anything you happened to overhear is really none of your business."

Hurt sliced through her. "I overheard it, as you so

nicely put it, because I was worried sick about you and doing my best to bring your fever down.'' Her movements jerky and agitated, she tossed the pasta in the pot of boiling water. "So am I seeing the real man now? Is this what you're normally like? As crabby as a rattlesnake when someone gets too close?''

"You've got one hell of a temper.''

"I'm the one who wants to keep my hair tied back. Red hair, as you've noticed.''

The words were dragged from him. "Is it really that color?''

"Oh, no. I'm a blue-eyed blonde.''

"Okay, okay, so I got out of bed in a foul mood! I don't want to hang around here any longer than necessary, Morgan. Quite apart from our safety—assuming Howard and his rifle are still roaming around on the loose—I'm supposed to meet someone in Salt Lake City tomorrow. Someone important enough that I've driven here all the way from California.''

"Then you're going to be late. Although if you'd stop being so ridiculously overprotective, I could go into Sorel and at least make a phone call for you.'' She frowned. "This meeting in Salt Lake City—could it have anything to do with Howard and Dez?''

His hesitation was so brief she might have imagined it. "It's too far-fetched to even think that...we're snatching at straws.''

He wasn't telling her what the meeting was about, Morgan noticed, and said snappishly, "Straws are all we've got and I do wish you'd let me go for help.''

"No! And don't try sneaking off when I'm not looking, will you, Morgan? Because I'll come after you.''

"Just because we're camped on a ledge, you don't have to behave like a caveman.''

"I don't understand how the devil I've been behaving since I met you!''

"How about arrogant and overbearing?" she said sweetly.

"You have to be the lippiest woman I've ever come across."

With the air of one making a discovery, Morgan said, "You know what? You bring out the absolute worst in me—I'm not normally lippy. Not with strange men, anyway. That's weird."

For the first time Riley's mouth relaxed into something near a smile. "Weird and mutual. You definitely bring out the worst in me, Morgan Cassidy."

"I wonder why?"

"I don't want to know," he responded grimly.

It was odd, considering the tenor of their conversation, how alive she felt. Vibrantly alive. Morgan raised one brow. "Well. So you're a coward. I wouldn't have suspected that of you."

"As far as you're concerned, yes, I'm an arrant coward."

Nor would she have expected him to admit it. Further discovering that she was thoroughly enjoying herself, Morgan tested a piece of the pasta and adjusted the burner to simmer. "We've already established I'm in no way your physical equal. So you're not afraid I'll beat up on you. What else could it possibly be?"

He said amiably, "Perhaps I'm afraid your tongue will flay the skin off my back."

"Are you as protective of Anna as you are of me?"

His jaw tensed. "That, my dear Morgan, remains my secret. You'd better hope I heal fast. Because I can see this being a very long three days."

Her mother and father had never had a conversation like this in their lives. So why was she so exhilarated?

Reason after reason tumbled through Morgan's brain. Riley doesn't back down. He's a worthy opponent. He's intelligent and subtle and full of secrets.

Nothing to do with his sexiness, though. The breadth of his shoulders, the blue depths of his eyes, his strongly carved mouth: they're irrelevant. Totally irrelevant.

"You look very fierce," Riley said, amused.

She stared at him in dismay. What about his smile, Morgan? A smile that makes your heart jump around like a newborn mule deer. "I think the pasta's ready," she said loudly. "I'll get you a plate."

And if that wasn't a retreat, she didn't know what it was.

Riley ate everything she'd put on his plate. Morgan could tell his appetite wasn't great, that he was forcing himself to eat to get his strength back. So he could leave all the sooner, she thought peevishly, and disappeared to get water for dishes. When she came back she explained about the tanks, the eroded holes at the base of the cliff where water collected. "It's good enough for washing dishes and ourselves. I have a filter I use when my water bottles run out. That way I never have to go into town once I'm settled in camp."

She offered him an orange and cleaned up the campsite, the candlelight caught in her hair so it glowed like the embers of a fire. He said, rubbing his jaw, "I don't suppose you have a razor?" She shook her head. "Then I guess you'll have to put up with me looking like a third-rate gangster. I could do with a wash, though."

"I'll heat some water for you."

"Thanks." He looked her in the eye. "The day after tomorrow, Morgan. That's when we'll leave."

"We'll see," she said, her chin tilted defiantly.

"Yes," he said in a steel voice, "we will."

She plunked the pot of water on the stove, laid out a towel and soap, and went for a walk down the streambed in the moonlight. She felt as edgy as a coyote in mating season, she thought crossly, wondering if it would help to howl at the moon. Then her steps slowed, and she began scuffing in the dirt with the toe of her boot. What she didn't feel—right now, at least—was the dead weight of the exhaustion she'd labored under for the last thirteen months.

Somehow Riley had banished that.

Riley? Or the way she felt around Riley?

She wished she knew who Anna was.

She kicked at the nearest rock. You're behaving like one of your own students, Morgan! It's very simple. You came here to be alone and you're not alone. So you're cranky and irritable. That's all. All this feeling alive guff—you're kidding yourself. So what if you've gotten to know Riley's body rather too well? So what if his temperament strikes sparks off your own? Once he's gone, you'll forget him.

Of course you will.

Rather pleased with herself for having figured all this out, Morgan strolled back to the campsite, stopping occasionally to lift her face to the remote majesty of the stars. When she got back to the tent, the little candles were still burning and the tent flap was closed. Riley had gone to bed.

She had a wash herself, feeling her spirits settle into the slowness that all ordinary tasks took when she was camping. A slowness she needed after the last few months in Boston.

Then she unzipped the flap and got into the tent. Riley was asleep, his bare back firmly turned toward her. For a split second she was struck by the beauty of design of muscle and bone, of curves and planes and hard angles that were indisputably and wholly male. Then she tossed her head and crouched down, pulling on her T-shirt and pulling off her boots and trousers. She lay down, turned her back on Riley and composed herself for sleep.

*   *   *

Somehow the boundary between dream and wakefulness had dissolved. Morgan lay very still. Her cheek was resting on what appeared to be Riley's shoulder. He was rhythmically stroking her hair. In her ear reverberated the strong, steady pounding of his heart. Was this a continuation of a dream she'd been having that had been suffused with the smooth, heated slide of flesh against flesh? Or was she truly awake?

Her arm was draped across his chest, the roughness of his body hair tickling her skin. It was that tickling sensation that decided her. She was awake, she thought in sudden panic. This was no dream. It was real.

Very slowly she opened her eyes.

In the night they had turned to each other, he to her and she to him. She said in a choked whisper, "Riley...what are we *doing*?"

"Hush," he said softly, and cupped her shoulder in his hand. Her breasts were pressed to his ribs, and the heat of the dream and the heat of reality had spread all through her body so that her limbs felt heavy and languorous and her breasts pulsed with sweetness. Instinctively she burrowed a little closer, and began stroking the taut hollow in his belly where his rib cage converged, where the muscles were banded and tight.

He said with that lazy humor that she found so attractive, "You're not the only one who did weights last winter."

She glanced up at him. His face was gentled and open to her in a way that was new. Yet his eyes were blazingly blue, like the sky that arched over the limestone cliffs day after day, year after year. She watched him bring his head down to hers, his intent as clearly to be read as a desert horizon. Her lashes drifted to her cheeks as she felt the first brush of his lips against hers.

It was a kiss that began with a kind of dreamlike sensuality. Yet within it from the beginning were the seeds of intensity; Riley pulled her closer, his mouth moving back and forth across hers with a deliberate restraint that was infinitely arousing. Knowing she had no choice, Morgan lifted to meet him, her hair tumbling forward to enclose his face. He buried his free hand in its vivid curls and deepened his kiss, teasing her lips open, seeking the dance of her tongue.

That first touch of his tongue to hers was for Morgan as dramatic and uncontrollable as a streak of lightning from clouds piled high over the mesa. Her whole body ignited to its fire, so that she forgot everything but its primitive, elemental energy. And that, too, was new to her.

Then Riley heaved himself half out of the sleeping bag. She fell back on her pillow, from a long way away sensing him flinch as he moved his injured leg. Closer, much closer, was the weight of his body over hers, the thrust of her breasts against his torso, his intimate invasion of her mouth. She wrapped her arms around his neck and held him tight, and heard him groan her name deep in his throat. Then his hand fumbled for the hem of her shirt and slid beneath it.

All the heat of the desert was in the touch of his fingers. She felt them seek out, strong and sure, the swell of her breast with its rock-hard tip and gave a cry of sheer delight. As though this were all the catalyst he needed, he roughly hauled her shirt over her head, his eyes drinking in the ivory beauty of her body. "You're so beautiful," he breathed, "and I want you so much— God, I've never wanted a woman like this."

She, she thought dazedly, had never in her life responded to a man with such frantic and wanton immediacy. Never. Had never realized that for her the possibility even existed. "Me, too," she mumbled incoherently and ungrammatically, and realized something else: she didn't want to talk or think. She wanted

Riley. In the most basic way possible between a man and a woman. She pulled his head down and kissed him with an ardor that was both unpracticed and obviously sincere.

He shoved the sleeping bag lower on her hips and pulled her toward him. ''Morgan,'' he muttered against her mouth, ''any minute now we're not going to be able to stop—are you okay with this?''

''Yes, oh yes!''

''You're protected?''

''Yes, of course I—*what* did you say?''

He kissed the tip of her nose, clearly confident of her reply. ''Protected. Against pregnancy. I have a clean bill of health, by the way…sorry this all sounds so unromantic, but this is the nineties.''

''No,'' she said blankly. ''I'm not protected. Why would I be?''

''You're not on the pill?''

''No. I told you, I'm not involved with anyone, there's been no need for me to worry about getting pregnant.''

Aghast, she bit her lip. The dream had shattered around her in a thousand pieces, and she was left with a reality that appalled her. She, Morgan, was half naked in the embrace of a man she'd met less than forty-eight hours ago, a man who was virtually a stranger to her. How could she have behaved like this?

She scrabbled for her T-shirt, avoiding his eyes. But he stayed her hand, saying harshly, ''You've got nothing to be ashamed of.''

''Let *go*!'' Distraught, she tried to yank free. ''I *never* behave like this. Never. I don't know what happened to me, I must have been out of my mind.''

''We both were,'' he said curtly. ''You're not telling me you're a virgin?''

''No! Let go, Riley, please.''

Reluctantly he released her wrist. "There's no need to be so upset."

"Maybe you do this sort of thing all the time," she said nastily, her voice muffled as she hauled her shirt over her head, "but I don't."

"Stop it," he said jaggedly. "I'm no more used to this situation than you are. After all, if I went around seducing every woman I came across, I'd be traveling with my own protection, wouldn't I? But when I woke up this morning, you were lying half on top of me, and your hair smelled so sweet and you were warm and—hell, I don't have to spell it out, you're a big girl. It won't happen again, Morgan, I swear it won't."

"You're darn right it won't," she said furiously, not even caring that he could see her bare legs as she dragged her bush pants up over her thighs.

"I don't want to get involved any more than you do!"

"Maybe we will leave here tomorrow. For me, it can't be too soon."

Riley said with dangerous softness, "You liked it, Morgan. Don't forget that."

"Oh, shut *up*!" she cried, lacing her boots on all the wrong holes, her fingers trembling. "I'm going to get breakfast. You can do what you like."

Morgan practically dived out of the tent, banging her knees on the rock. The fact that it was a perfect day outside made her feel even worse. Her mood called for thunderheads and the gray slash of rain, not an umblemished sky the exact color of Riley's eyes and a warmth on her face like the heat of his skin. Damn, damn, damn, she raged, thumping her fist fruitlessly on the boulder beside her stove. If only I could undo the last hour. Make it never to have happened.

She couldn't do that. But she could darn well pretend it hadn't happened. To herself or to Riley.

*   *   *

The day passed with excruciating slowness. Morgan read her book, ostentatiously sitting as far from the tent and from Riley as she could. In the afternoon she went for a long walk in the direction opposite to the highway, and the whole time failed miserably to erase the memory of that early morning lovemaking from her mind. Or from her body.

Every little thing served to remind her. The burnished streaks on the limestone cliffs were as dark as Riley's hair. The sinuous curves of erosion became the elegant curve of his shoulder, their shadowed depressions like the hollows above his collarbones. Even the day's drowsy heat cast a spell achingly similar to the one he'd cast over her with the sureness of his touch and the depth of his kisses. She couldn't escape him, no matter which way she turned. With her whole being she longed for the blue of the sky to be swallowed by dusk.

How was she going to share the tent with him tonight?

Why had she never felt this way with Chip? Or with Tomas, the young man who'd relieved her of her virginity her second year at university. Painlessly, but not memorably.

If she made love with Riley, she'd remember it. Every detail.

She stormed back to the camp, her mood not helped when she saw Riley limping back and forth along the ledge in an obvious effort to strengthen his torn muscles. So he could get out of here tomorrow.

Hardening her heart against the dark shadows under his eyes and the lines of pain engraved around his mouth, she heated some stew, adding freeze-dried vegetables and making tea biscuits out of a prepared mix and powdered milk. "Supper's ready," she called ungraciously.

He hobbled over and took the heaped plate from her, eating in a silence that further infuriated her. As he scraped the plate clean, he said, "That was good, Morgan. Thanks."

The timbre of his voice shivered through her. Face it, Morgan, it wouldn't matter if he never said a word or talked nonstop, you'd still be as cross as the proverbial bear. You just don't want to be anywhere in his vicinity. "You're welcome," she said stiffly and without much regard for truth.

He said in a flat voice, "I'll sleep outside tonight."

She glared at him. "You will not. I haven't come this far to let you be poisoned by a rattlesnake."

"I have yet to lay eyes on a single snake."

"I saw two rattlers further down the gully this afternoon. And they like the moisture at the end of the ledge. You'll sleep in the tent, Riley."

"You know what?" he snarled. "I have a very hard time taking orders from you."

"Name one man who likes taking orders from a woman," she flashed. "Once I deposit you in Sorel, you can do what you please. But until then, I'm the one who knows about the desert and I call the shots."

She could see frustration and rage clamping his jaw-line and seething in his eyes; and with reluctant admiration watched him fight them down. He grated, "Then let's for heaven's sake call a truce. We're two adults, not a couple of squabbling teenagers."

"Oh, no," she said forcibly. "No truce. I don't want to share the tent with you any more than you want to share it with me."

"Fine," he snapped, and to her overwrought imagination it was as though ice had glazed his features and hardened his voice. "I'm going to bed."

Within minutes he had vanished inside the tent. Hunkered down near the stove, Morgan watched the currents swirl in the dishwater, bubbles rising to the surface, then bursting as though they'd never existed. She'd behaved with extraordinary childishness all day, she could admit that now that she was alone. But how else could she have handled a situation that was totally outside her experience? Or a man whose every small movement all day had inexorably brought her back to the image of their bodies lying together, skin to skin, hunger matching hunger?

For the first time since she'd been coming to the desert, Morgan found herself dreading the long hours of darkness.

CHAPTER FIVE

MORGAN didn't go to bed until at least midnight. All the usual wiles of the desert—stars, moon, silence and solitude—had failed to bring her peace. When she finally opened the tent flap, the scrape of the zipper sounded so loud that she winced inwardly. Riley's back was turned to her, just as it had been the night before, although tonight he'd covered his body completely with her sleeping bag, only his dark head visible. Every instinct she possessed told her that he was as wide awake as she was.

She had no intention of asking him if that were so.

She undressed, edged her own bag right to the wall of the tent and got in, burrowing her head into the folds of her fleece jacket. Then she lay still.

She couldn't hear him breathing.

She listened for several seconds, her eyes wideheld, panic stopping her own breath in her lungs, a panic so instant and instinctive she didn't stop to examine it. In a strangled voice she said, "Riley, are you okay?"

"Go to sleep."

He had snapped at her as if she were a naughty child. Her nostrils flared in the darkness, her temper not helped by the recognition that she was—once again—behaving childishly. "I couldn't hear you breathing and for a minute I thought—"

"You're the one who didn't want a truce, Morgan—so don't try for one now that we're both in bed."

His words flicked her on the raw. She hadn't wanted a truce, he was right. But did he now have to imply that she was trying to seduce him? Feeling cheapened and shamed, Morgan huddled lower into her sleeping bag, tears stinging her eyes.

The man who had just spoken to her was the same man who, after she had first cleaned his wound, had intuited her storm of weeping and had comforted her in his embrace. With genuine tenderness, she would have sworn.

It was quite clear he didn't feel tender toward her now. The exact opposite, in fact. More tears slid down her cheeks, silent and purposeful tears, springing from a hurt whose source she wasn't sure she understood. How had she admitted Riley Hanrahan so deeply into her life that she was now vulnerable to him?

Not only how, but why?

Argue and ask questions, that's all I've done in the last two days, Morgan thought unhappily. He's destroyed my solitude and banished my peace. But tomorrow he'll be gone.

Hold on to that thought, Morgan. Tomorrow Riley will vanish from your life as abruptly as he entered it.

Tomorrow wasn't soon enough.

Morgan did sleep, although it was a fitful sleep shot through with bizarre dreams that culminated in a nightmare. A woman named Anna was chasing her down endless corridors, brandishing a bone-handled knife whose blade gleamed silver; and all the while Riley, Howard and Dez stood on the sidelines and watched. Grinning and guzzling beer.

As she was about to tumble down a flight of stairs flanked by huge figures in rusty suits of armor, Morgan woke with a smothered gasp of terror.

"For Pete's sake, what's wrong?"

In utter confusion Morgan gaped at Riley. "You wouldn't help me," she accused. "You just stood there smirking while that woman did her best to murder me."

"You were dreaming," he said impatiently.

At least they hadn't been erotic dreams. That much she'd been spared. Although, once again, she and Riley were face-to-face in the all-too-narrow space of the tent. "I'm going to get up," she snapped. "Turn your back."

Overnight the weather had changed, the sky heaped with ominously fat cumulus clouds, the wind chill on her face. Shivering, she went for water. She had breakfast under way by the time Riley awkwardly climbed out of the tent. As she stirred raisins and dried apricots into the oatmeal, she watched him doggedly limping the length of the ledge and back again. Limping hard, she thought, and turned the burner off under the coffeepot. "Coffee's ready," she called.

He was leaning one hand against the overhang, his chest heaving. She stirred the oatmeal rather more than it needed and reached for his mug, filling it with the steaming, fragrant brew. As he hobbled over to her, she added the two heaped spoons of sugar that she knew he liked, and stirred in dried cream. He sank down on the nearest boulder and she passed him the mug of coffee.

"Thanks, Morgan."

Her eyes skittered away from his. As she lowered the flame under the oatmeal and started mixing some powdered milk, he said brusquely, "How far do we have to walk to get to your car?"

"About four miles. We'll have to double back, you see."

"What's the going like?"

"Much the same as it was on the way in. Rough enough."

He put his mug down very carefully on the rock. "I'll never make it. Not today. Because I'm damned if I'm going to lean on you for the whole four miles."

His jaw was tense, his mouth a gash in a face closed to her. Her heart sank. She wasn't sure she could stand another twenty-four hours like the last twenty-four. "I don't mind if you lean on me," she lied.

"I do."

Some of the milk sloshed over the edge of the pan. Morgan struggled to contain her temper and said evenly, "I'd much rather we go today."

"Do you think I don't feel the same way? Of course I do! But I'm also old enough to know my limitations."

The words tumbled from nowhere. "Am I so awful that you can't wait to be rid of me?" she cried, and felt raw pain close her throat.

Riley let out his breath in a long sigh. "Hell, Morgan...do I have to spell it out for you? I want to make love to you so badly that being within fifty feet of you is like a very refined form of torture. I lay awake the whole night and right now I'd like to haul you off to the tent like the caveman you compared me to. I've never in my life felt this way—so out of control, so much at the mercy of another human being. And I hate it, just in case you hadn't guessed." Ruefully he gave her the lopsided smile that never failed to move her. "I'm behaving with about as much subtlety as a bull moose in rutting season, I know. For that, I apologize. The rest I can't help. Although I swear I won't lay a finger on you."

It had been a very comprehensive speech. In a dazed voice Morgan said, "Do you want some oatmeal?"

"Is that your best offer?"

And what was she supposed to say to that? Her fingers wrapping themselves around the wooden spoon so hard that her knuckles were white as bone, she asked, "Riley, who's Anna?"

He grimaced. "Did I talk about her a lot?"

She nodded and added with a sudden, sly grin, "She was the one who was chasing me with a butcher knife when I woke up this morning."

"So you're not immune to me."

Morgan stared at him. "Did you think I was?"

"Yesterday you did a darn good job of convincing me you were. And yes, I'll have some oatmeal."

Some of the tension had eased from his shoulders. Her lower lip caught in her teeth, her brow furrowed in thought, Morgan dished out the oatmeal and passed him milk and syrup. She said, gazing at her bowl as though she'd never seen anything as fascinating as the lumpy gray cereal, "The way I've felt in the last two days, it's totally new for me, too, and I've got nothing to compare it with. I thought I knew myself and now suddenly I've found out I don't." She glanced up, her eyes very green. "If you're a bull moose, I'm a newborn deer—leaping all over the map without a speck of grace."

He said with sudden intensity, "Your grace is one of the things that catches at my heart."

Morgan choked on a mouthful of oatmeal and flushed scarlet. She said foolishly, "I don't even know how old you are."

"Thirty-five. Anna, by the way, was a nun."

Morgan dropped her spoon. "A *nun*?"

"Sister Anna. A tiny woman with golden-brown eyes, the energy of a dynamo and the kindest heart in the world. She and five other sisters ran a small orphanage in New York City, and that's where I grew up. My parents were Irish, and died in a train crash. But before you start feeling sorry for me, let me add that the nuns were wonderful and I was very happy there. Even if I was heartily in awe of Mother Superior."

Morgan's emotions were running the gamut between an overwhelming gratitude and intense curiosity. Her brain in overdrive, she asked, "How many children in the orphanage?"

"Roughly seventy."

"So the nuns would have been very busy."

"What are you getting at?"

"When you were feverish, you said someone was too busy for you...it sounded painful."

"When I was a kid, I used to have nightmares," he said in a clipped voice. "One night I wanted Anna, and Mother Superior told me Sister Anna was much too busy to be bothered with a silly dream."

"How old were you?"

"Four or five. I told you not to feel sorry for me, Morgan. Whatever I've made of myself, I owe to those nuns."

Sensing she'd been given the key to his character, needing to be alone to figure it out, Morgan announced with a toss of her head, "Stop telling me what I'm supposed to feel."

"All my adult life," he said tightly, "my preference has been for women who are calm and serene. Like the sisters, I suppose...you don't need a degree in psychology to figure that one out."

"I want a man who's as even-tempered as my father, and a marriage that's as calm and affectionate as his with my mother."

"So it's only sex between us."

She didn't like the relief in his voice. Not one bit. "There's nothing calm about you and me."

"Hormones, Morgan. Together with, in my case, a long spell of abstinence."

"And was sex with that last woman calm and serene, too?"

Morgan hadn't known she was going to ask that. Riley said, his eyes sparking with laughter, "Actually, it was deadly dull."

"That would pretty well describe Tomas and Chip, too."

"So we're into True Confessions, are we? It wouldn't be dull between you and me."

It was as though Riley had reached out and physically stroked her. Refusing to back down, Morgan said, "No, I don't think it would be."

"I'm damn sure it wouldn't be." His eyes narrowed. "So...when we get out of here, are we going to put that to the test?"

"No," she gasped, and sought for a reason. "I don't know the first thing about you."

"I think you know a great deal. As I do about you. Your courage, your independence, your temper. Your incredible beauty. We've cut to the essentials, the things that count. The rest—where we live, what we do—that's just window dressing."

With the sense that she was caught in quicksand, Morgan said forcefully, "Riley, once I deliver you to Sorel, I'm coming back here. Alone."

"Not if I can help it."

Her bowl appeared to be empty and she had no recollection of having eaten anything. Agitated, she burst out, "I studied psychology, I know about sex drives. What's happened in the last couple of days is pure melodrama—shootings and blood and sleeping together in a tent in the wilderness. No wonder our hormones are rampant. But it's got nothing to do with real life. With yours or with mine." Scrambling to her feet, she made a parting shot. "You said yourself you didn't want to get involved. So we won't. And now I'm going for a walk. A long one."

She set off down the gully as if a pack of coyotes was in pursuit of her. At least Riley couldn't come after her, she was glad of that. One kiss from him and all her high-sounding rhetoric, she was ninety-nine percent sure, would dissolve into mush. As would she.

So keep your distance, Morgan, she told herself, and lengthened her stride.

She walked for a long time, although she was, contrary to her usual practice, almost oblivious to her surroundings. Somehow she was caught up in the vision of a little boy who'd needed comfort in the night and had been denied it. A boy who'd been one of many in the care of women who, no matter how good-hearted, must have been overworked.

Intimacy, she thought, her steps slowing. That's what he would have been denied. Could detached be an alternate word for calm and serene?

Chip had been detached. So, in essence, had Tomas. Yet at the time she'd thought she was intimate with them.

And what of her parents' calm and peaceful marriage? Was that intimacy? Or was it merely a facade?

More questions, she thought crossly, and unclipped her canteen to have a drink. For the first time in quite a while she looked around her, and with a jolt of fear that banished any cogitations on intimacy saw a multicolored rainbow arching from horizon to horizon, and behind it a great curtain of rain obscuring the limestone cliffs. With another jolt, fear was transformed to terror. She hadn't warned Riley about flash floods. What if he'd gone for a walk in the streambed? He'd never get out in time.

She began to run, darting over the uneven terrain with a speed that in cold blood she wouldn't have contemplated. She'd never forgive herself if anything happened to Riley. Why, oh why, when she'd seen the clouds this morning, hadn't she warned him?

As she ran, her ears were straining for another sound. Twice in her desert sojourns Morgan had seen—and heard—flash floods; their approach had reminded her of the faraway sounds of traffic on a highway at rush hour. Leaping from boulder to boulder with a supple grace that Riley would have recognized, her eyes seeking always the quickest path, she sprinted up the streambed. Why had she come so far? And what an abysmally stupid thing to do, to abandon her normal watchfulness.

Her boots were scrunching among the loose stones, and for a moment she stopped, trying to quiet the pounding of her heart and her rapid breathing to listen for a different sound. And then in stark horror she heard it: that distant rumble that someone who knew no better would never have thought was water.

She took off like a bullet from a gun, screaming Riley's name at the top of her lungs. The cliff walls flung it back to her in an echo full of mockery. Two more turns in the streambed and she'd be at the ledge…if he wasn't there, she'd have to keep going. Pain stabbed her side, and grimly she ignored it. He had to be safe. He *had* to be.

She rounded the final corner and screamed his name again.

The ledge was empty.

With a moan of sheer dread Morgan raced past the first rise in the rock face. "Riley!" she yelled. "Riley, where are you?"

"What's the matter?" he said.

She stumbled to a halt and saw what she hadn't noticed moments earlier. The tent flap was open. Riley was edging out onto the ledge, favoring his leg, getting to his feet with a clumsy lurch. She stood still, one hand clasping the stitch in her chest, and felt the world tilt beneath her feet. He was safe.

Then she realized something else: that the flash flood was nearer. Appreciably nearer. Galvanized into action, she scrabbled up the rock face, the toes of her boots and her fingernails searching for purchase; with one final heave she reached the safety of the ledge and pulled herself upright. Not even stopping to think, she threw herself at Riley, wrapped her arms around his waist with all her remaining strength and buried her face in his shoulder. Automatically his own arms went around her. "What's the matter?" he said in a peculiar voice. "Why were you yelling my name?"

Her arms tightened their hold. His shirt smelled of desert air and sweat, his skin smelled of soap, and through the thrumming of her pulse she was aware only of the deepest gratitude that he was out of danger. She muttered into his collarbone, "Flash flood. Hear it?"

"All I can hear is your heartbeat," he said roughly.

"Listen!"

He paused. "You mean that sound we can hear, it's water?"

"A lot of water. If you get caught in a streambed in a flash flood, you're a goner." She suddenly looked up, her eyes anguished. "I didn't warn you. This morning when I saw the look of the sky, I should have warned you. But I didn't. I was too intent on putting as much distance between you and me as I could. Riley, I'd never have forgiven myself if—"

"I was as much responsible for what went on this morning as you were. My God, Morgan, listen to it."

They were both looking up the canyon when, like a mud-brown battering ram, a great wave thrust its way between the rocks. In its vanguard an uprooted tree trunk cartwheeled its limbs like a clown gone mad. Then the gully disappeared beneath a welter of churning, opaque water. Boulders battered the ledge; logs were tossed like matchsticks.

Over the roar of water Riley said incredulously, "Where the hell did it come from, all that water?"

Morgan clutched him all the harder. "I was so afraid you'd have gone for a walk up the canyon. That you'd be trapped and drowned—I couldn't have borne that."

He drew her further away from the edge. "Are you trying to tell me that if I hadn't been on the ledge, you'd have gone up the gully looking for me?"

She stated the obvious. "Of course I would."

"Morgan..." She couldn't possibly have deciphered the expression on his face as he pulled her hard against him and kissed her parted lips. But the kiss she knew. Knew and welcomed and responded to with passionate thankfulness that she was in his arms and he was safe. However, as fiercely as the flood behind her back, gratitude changed to something else, something more complex and compelling, something to which she opened in pure delight.

Her trembling limbs, her tiny moans of pleasure, her pliant surrender to a flood of desire as Riley found the swell of her breast beneath her shirt, were all part of this complexity. She fumbled with the buttons on his shirt and thrust one hand to play with the tangled hair of his chest, feeling the heat of his skin, the sudden tautness of his belly. She tugged at his waistband, only wanting flesh pressed to flesh, with no barriers. And that, too, was part of the complexity.

He stilled her hand. "Morgan, we can't!"

His eyes were burning right through her, blue as the skies she'd been returning to, summer after summer. "But I want—"

He put a finger to her mouth, gently rubbing her lips' softness, and at the same time moving his hips against hers. "I do, too—no way I can hide it. But we can't. Not now. We can't risk starting a child neither of us wants."

And how's that last statement for complexity? she thought wildly, and felt her hips arch to his with a compulsion beyond her will. Roughly he pushed her away. "Don't!"

Her body sagged in his hold. "I can't stand this."

"Tomorrow," he said hoarsely. "Tomorrow we'll get out of here and we'll find a motel in Sorel and I'll make love to you the whole night through until neither one of us can stand up. Me or you.''

Morgan flinched away from the raw hunger in his face. She looked back over her shoulder, her feelings as tumultuous and impossible to read as the foam-ridden, muddy water; although the racket of the flood seemed to have subsided a little, unlike her feelings. "I'm coming back here tomorrow to be by myself," she said, and heard the words ripple through her head.

"We both know you're not going to do that."

She wasn't quite ready to admit that he might be right. "I saved your life—so I feel responsible for you. That's why I was so upset today."

His fingers dug into her shoulders. "No one's responsible for me but me, Morgan."

"All those serene, dull women, I bet they didn't feel responsible for you."

His mouth twisted in wry humor. "There weren't that many of them. And no, they didn't. Are you jealous, by any chance?"

"Of course not!"

"Your eyes look very green."

His crooked grin was irresistible. "Well," Morgan said, her own mouth curving in response, "maybe a little."

"The reason I haven't asked you about Tomas and Chip is because I want to punch them out." She blinked. "And could we please continue this sitting down? My leg hurts."

"There's nothing to continue," she said fretfully, plunking her behind on the nearest rock. "This is a ridiculous conversation! I made love with Tomas when I was nineteen, for goodness' sake."

Riley lowered himself on the same rock. Too close for comfort, thought Morgan, and heard him ask, "Was he the first?"

"And the last for a long time."

"Wasn't he good to you?" Riley exploded.

Startled, she said, "You know what? You look every bit as dangerous as a flash flood. He wasn't bad to me, Riley. It's just that…" She frowned, trying to project herself back ten years. "It was my second year at university, and I was much more interested in losing my virginity than I was in getting my term papers in on time. None of my friends were virgins, I was an anachronism and—I hate to say it—very much under the influence of peer pressure. So when I met Tomas at a frat house and we dated for a while, I persuaded myself I was in love with him and decided to go for broke." She scowled. "Since then I've learned to make my own decisions, regardless of my peers. It was okay, I guess. With Tomas. But I'd done a course on the romantic poets so I was expecting cataclysm. Stars moving, thunder and lightning, you know the kind of thing I mean." Her nose crinkled charmingly. "I was young for my age."

"No lightning?"

"Nary a flash."

"So what about Chip?"

She edged away from him. "Oh, that's another story. The water's going down, look."

His eyes didn't leave her face. "This thing you have for the desert—flash floods, rattlesnakes, scorpions and drought—is it a substitute for the kind of sex that you and I would have?"

She said testily, "Why don't you tell me what *you* do for excitement, Riley? Or is your whole life calm and serene?"

His eyes narrowed. "How about a fishing boat in a gale? Or deep-sea diving to free a dolphin trapped in a net? Or making underwater recordings of whale songs?"

She said uncertainly, "You're a scientist?"

"I research the migratory patterns of whales."

"I figured it was something like that," she said slowly. "Surfing the big ones in Hawaii. Skiing in front of avalanches. You've got that look about you." Even more slowly she went on, "So you go to the ocean, whereas I go to the desert…we're as different as night and day, you and I. One more reason for me to come back here tomorrow night."

He put his hand on her thigh. "I love the ocean the way you love the desert. For its beauty and its dangers. We're very much the same, Morgan. Neither of us wants to live without risk."

The weight of his palm burned through her trousers. And what was that if not a risk? Flustered, Morgan stood up. "You live in California and I live in Boston, and one lasting lesson I learned from Tomas was not to indulge in casual sex."

"I live in Maine. I run a research station there, and contract out to trawlers when whales get caught in their nets. Maine's not that far from Massachusetts." His voice unrelenting, he added, "Sex doesn't have to mean marriage. But sex between you and me would never be casual."

"You figure if we make love, then you'll be immune to me? Sex as a glorified flu shot?"

"I'm not that naive, Morgan."

"All we do is fight!"

"That's because we're two loners used to having our own way who've been thrown into a kind of intimacy we both abhor."

"Abhor. That's a strong word." A word she disliked. Not that she was going to tell him that.

"I say it like I see it."

"So this sex we're talking about—it's not going to be casual, but it's not going to last and it's not going to be intimate. Forgive me if I'm a little confused."

He shoved himself to his feet. "You think I've got it all figured out?" he blazed. "I did use the word risk."

"I hate this!" she shouted back. "Is it intimacy you abhor or is it me?"

"Don't be coy," he snarled. "You infuriate me, you arouse me, and in three days you've turned my world upside down. But no, I don't abhor you, Morgan Cassidy."

"There's times I sympathize with Howard," she said darkly. "Homicide and all."

As Riley threw back his head and laughed, his teeth gleaming white against his tanned skin, Morgan realized with a judder of surprise that once again she felt fully and vibrantly alive. And again it wasn't the desert making her feel that way. It was a man.

The sexiest man she'd ever met. Also the most obstreperous.

"I'm going to make lunch," she said grumpily. "Then you should have a rest if we're going to get out of here tomorrow."

"Yes, ma'am," he said meekly, and grinned at her.

She fought back an answering smile and wondered, oddly, and for the first time in her life, if perhaps fighting was a form of intimacy. Because why would you fight with someone if you didn't care about him?

CHAPTER SIX

THE day passed, and with it the rain. The gully and the debris left by the flood dried in the sun. Morgan prepared meals, washed dishes, braced herself to change the dressing on Riley's leg, and watched him carve a walking stick out of a piece of wood she'd brought him from among the mud-daubed stones; he whistled as he worked. She tried in vain to focus on her book.

Riley went to bed early. Morgan stayed up and thought about sex and intimacy and wondered what on earth she was going to do the next day. Certain that she'd never even close her eyes, she eventually moved to the tent and curled up in her sleeping bag, where she dropped instantly into a deep, dreamless sleep, and woke at daybreak to the sound of Riley's voice.

"Wake up, Morgan. Let's get out of here."

She sat up with a jounce, her breasts jiggling under her thin shirt. "It's morning already?"

He said gruffly, "Your hair's as wild as a storm at sea."

Mesmerized, she watched him curl one strand around his finger. "Did you sleep?" she muttered.

"After you came to bed, yes."

He sounded much like a husband might sound. She blurted, "I don't think I even know what intimacy is."

"More True Confessions?"

"Don't laugh at me!"

He tugged gently on her hair. "I wasn't meaning to. Morgan, I'm not sure I know what intimacy is, either. Although I suspect the fact that we're having this conversation has got something to do with it."

74

The question tripped from her tongue. "Riley, do you *like* me?"

"Very much."

"I like you, too," she said faintly, "although you do drive me crazy."

"Tell me about it," he remarked, releasing his hold on her hair. "Get up, woman. You've got to break camp and we need to hit the trail."

She hadn't even thought about her tent. If she took it down, it was a clear admission that she was staying with Riley in Sorel that night. She tossed her head, her hair a tangled swirl. "We've got a four-mile hike and I'm sure I'll have to help you some of the time. I can't do that and carry my backpack as well, it's too heavy."

"In that case," he said implacably, "you can stash your pack under the ledge. I daresay I wouldn't have been much use as a bodyguard the last couple of days, but I'm damned if you're coming back here on your own until I know that Howard and Dez are long gone. Anyway, I'm going to lay charges. So I'll need you as a witness."

Of course he'd lay charges, she realized. That was the whole point of going to the police. But why had she never thought through the consequences of telling the police about the shooting? "If Howard and Dez get caught, that could mean a trial," Morgan said, appalled. "I'll never be free of you."

The look on his face was anything but intimate. "Get up, Morgan," he growled. "Step one is to leave the campsite."

"We're fighting again," she said. All her fancy theories last night about fighting and intimacy were just that: theories. Theories that Riley was disproving and that she was going to keep to herself. She reached for her shirt and put it on over her T-shirt; and by working at top speed, she was ready to leave the ledge an hour and a half later.

Her gear was neatly stowed in a dry crevice. She and Riley had eaten breakfast, and each of them was carrying a full canteen and snacks for the journey; she had put the first-aid kit in her small haversack along with a change of clothes.

Morgan took one last look around. The ledge looked very bare. She still couldn't quite believe she'd taken down her tent. That she was abandoning her campsite in favor of spending tonight in Sorel. With Riley.

In his bed or out of it?

"Let's go," she said.

Although she set a purposely slow pace for Riley's sake, she could feel his impatience nipping at her heels. Nevertheless, she insisted that they rest every twenty minutes or so, rests that became a little longer as they traversed the side canyon and the slickrock. By the time they'd crossed the third of a series of narrow canyons, Riley was leaning heavily on his makeshift walking stick; sweat beaded his forehead.

She said impetuously, "Lean on me for this next bit, Riley. We'll have to go around all those logs."

"I can manage," he rapped.

Fine, she thought. Fill your boots.

Furious with him for refusing her offer, furious with herself for minding, she stepped out ahead of him into the glare of sunshine, her attention on anything but where she was putting her feet. She heard a rattle, that unmistakable warning signal, and simultaneously saw a flash of movement: the gaping jaws and wickedly curved canines of the rattlesnake imprinted themselves on her brain. Then she was grabbed from behind, lifted off her feet and dumped with scant ceremony ten feet away from the snake. Taking its time, the rattler slithered under the log, leaving coiled, delicately sculpted tracks in the sand.

Riley brought her around to face him and said urgently, "Did it get you?"

"N-no," she stuttered.

"Was it a rattlesnake?"

She nodded. "A midget faded rattlesnake," she said with careful accuracy.

"I didn't think it was very big...did I overreact?"

"Oh, no. Its venom is one of the highest on the toxicity scale." Morgan shivered, looking straight at him. "Your leg might be in bad shape. But there's nothing wrong with your reflexes. You got me out of a bad spot—thanks, Riley."

He was rubbing his thigh. "A hurricane at sea's going to seem like a piece of cake after this place."

She said truthfully, "That was my fault. I wasn't paying attention, and snakes often lie in the sun by logs and rocks when the cooler weather starts."

"My fault, too," he said heavily. "I was the one who refused your help. How about we declare a truce at least until we get to the car? That way we might both get out of here alive."

"Did it hurt your leg, picking me up like that?"

"Didn't help it."

"Riley, I'm sorry." She bit her lip, seeing new lines of pain scoring his face. "Another two hours and we'll be out of here." With a wobbly smile she added, "Just imagine, motels come with hot showers."

"And beds," he said, dropping a kiss on her nose.

"By the look of you right now, my virtue won't be at risk."

"I wouldn't count on it," he said softly.

She made an indecipherable sound, placed his hand firmly on her shoulder and led him in a wide detour of the sun-warmed logs.

*   *   *

Two and a half hours later Morgan and Riley were edging through the cottonwoods toward Morgan's car. Sunlight and shadow danced through the golden leaves, which rustled their secrets to the wind. The swish of passing cars for once fell agreeably on Morgan's ears; Riley, she knew, was near the end of his tether. She said quietly, "You stay here. I'm going to check on my car—I left hairs in the doors so I'd know if anyone had tampered with it."

"The FBI should hire you," Riley said, and leaned against the nearest tree.

The hairs were just where she'd left them. Quickly she unlocked her car, threw her pack in the back, and helped Riley into the passenger seat. Then she drove onto the highway. "A rusty red truck, that's what they were driving," she said, and accelerated as fast as she could.

But although Morgan kept checking in the rearview mirror, she didn't see Howard's red truck. Riley's eyes were shut. He looked exhausted. A doctor, she thought. That's first on the agenda. The police can wait.

As though he'd read her mind, Riley said succinctly, "Find the police station first and let's get that over with."

"By the look of you, a doctor should be the priority."

"Police, Morgan."

Chewing on her lip, she headed for the main street, and ten minutes later they were telling their story to the officer on duty. He wasn't impressed with either one of them, being of the opinion that Morgan should have reported the incident four days ago and that Riley should have been more cautious in hunting season. "Your car was reported abandoned, Mr. Hanrahan, we impounded it this morning. Next step would've bin a search party. Big expense and bigger headache."

Riley said levelly, "Have you seen the red truck that Miss Cassidy described to you?"

"Not a sign of it."

Laboriously he started taking down particulars. He doesn't believe a word we've told him, Morgan decided, and heard him ask Riley, "Nature of your business in Salt Lake City?"

Riley hesitated. "It's a legal matter."

"Anythin' to do with this attempted homicide?"

Again Riley hesitated. "I can't imagine so, no."

"A legal matter...you own land in these parts?"

"No. It's to do with a will."

"Name of deceased?"

"I can't see that this is relevant."

"Mister, someone shot you in the leg and left you out there in the desert to die. Must've bin a reason, and in my experience most crimes come down to plain old dollars and cents." He scratched his jaw and repeated, "Name of deceased?"

"Beth Slater," Riley said.

For the first time the policeman cracked a smile. "You find out you've inherited a million bucks from this broad, you let us know. Then we'd have ourselves a dandy motive for a shootin'."

Morgan gazed fixedly at the Wanted posters, although afterward she couldn't have described a single one of the faces. Who was Beth Slater? And why had Riley never mentioned her name?

A few minutes later they went outdoors into the sunshine. "I forgot to ask him where the hospital is," Morgan said edgily. "I'll be right back."

Riley grabbed her wrist. "I hate hospitals—have ever since I had my appendix out when I was nine. Book us into the best motel in town, Morgan, and I'll call my friend Mike, he's a doctor here in Sorel. We went to college together, I drove this way especially to see him.

He'll come to the motel and look after me there. I hate
fuss even more than I hate hospitals.''

''You sure are stubborn,'' she said irritably, and
helped him back into the car. They drove off. Noticeably
she said nothing more. Not because she had nothing to
say, but because she had far too much. Riley was drum-
ming his fingers on his knee; he was not normally a man
for idle gestures.

Yet why should it matter to her who Beth Slater was?
She could be an elderly philanthropist leaving money for
whale research; and Riley, in all fairness, had had other
things on his mind since the shooting besides some old
lady's will.

All of which admirably rational thinking only very
slightly calmed the turmoil lodged somewhere between
Morgan's stomach and her heart.

She parked near the office of her favorite motel in
Sorel, the one whose restaurant had an excellent chef
and whose rooms had tiny patios opening onto a court-
yard of shrubs and trees. Riley fumbled in his pack and
passed her a credit card. ''Book the best room in the
place,'' he said.

She could have argued. She could have told him to
keep his money, she liked to pay her own way. She
could have lectured him on female independence. ''All
right,'' she said.

Because if she'd saved his life, he, today, had almost
certainly saved hers. Which had nothing to do with Beth
Slater.

Ten minutes later she was ushering him into a room
that overlooked palm trees and potted begonias on a se-
cluded patio. The room was decorated in restful shades
of rose and sage green, the plush carpet a deeper green.
The two queen-size beds had floral comforters in the
same colors; the bathroom, Morgan saw in one quick
peek was luxuriously appointed. Riley sat down on the

nearest bed and picked up the phone. "I'll get hold of Mike. Then I have to call Salt Lake City."

"Maybe I'll have a shower, then," Morgan said, grabbed her pack and headed for the bathroom.

The complimentary soap, shampoo and body lotion were wonderfully scented. When she emerged, feeling very much like a new woman in clean bush pants and a blue shirt, her hair in an unruly cloud around her head, Riley was propped up on the bed, reading. He said with a casualness she should have welcomed but that irked her no end, "I'm not going to kiss you, not until I have a shower. Mike should be here within the hour. I wondered in the meantime if you'd mind buying me something to wear, Morgan, I'm sick of this shirt and my jeans are only fit for the wastebasket. I made a list."

He didn't sound remotely like the passionate man whose every touch had set her pulses rocketing. "Sure," Morgan said coolly.

She went outside and as she unlocked the car door, glanced through the list. Clothes, then toilet articles, nothing very…her eyes widened and the paper twitched in her fingers. The last item on the list was condoms.

How dare he? How *dare* he?

She got in the car, slammed the door and drove downtown. If Riley Hanrahan thought she was going to waltz into a drugstore and buy condoms, he was crazy. She'd never done that in her life and she wasn't going to start now.

If you don't, a little voice whispered in her ear, then you can't make love with him. It's that simple, Morgan. Besides, he can't very well walk to the drugstore. He can scarcely put one foot in front of the other.

That every word of this was true did nothing to allay her fury at his effrontery. She jerked to a halt beside a parking meter and scrabbled for change in her wallet.

First things first. The man had to have a clean shirt and new jeans.

The only good thing about all this was that Beth Slater, whoever she was, was seeming less and less important.

Morgan spent half an hour in a clothing store picking out everything from jeans to jockey shorts. It seemed a very intimate thing to do, she thought, although not half as intimate as the next step.

The drugstore was next door. Toothpaste and a toothbrush, shaving cream, razor and blades, deodorant, one by one she put them in her basket. Then she stationed herself as nonchalantly as she could in front of the display labeled, euphemistically, "Men's Products."

The choice was overwhelming. Her cheeks scarlet, Morgan plucked four different color packages from the metal hooks, buried them beneath the razor blades and hurried to the counter. Once outside, she locked her purchases in the trunk and looked around.

She'd committed herself to making love with Riley. Hadn't she?

She felt as jumpy as a chipmunk, as restless as a baby deer. Perhaps it was this that drove her into a women's boutique, where she bought a gorgeous watered-silk nightgown. If she was going to take risks, she was going to darn well look her best while she did so.

When she got back to the motel, Dr. Mike Prescott had arrived before her. He was about Riley's age and height, with a thin, clever face, alert brown eyes and a thatch of auburn hair. "Riley and I are old college buddies," he explained as he finished taping Riley's leg. "I put in a couple of stitches. But you did a good job, Morgan—you don't mind if I call you that? Not a sign of infection."

Riley muttered, "After the way you poked around in

there, Mike, any self-respecting bug would have run the other way.''

He looked white about the mouth. His dark hair shone with cleanliness and he was clean-shaven; he was wearing a bath towel knotted around his waist and nothing else. Morgan said breathlessly, ''I got everything on the list, Riley.''

''Everything? Good for you,'' said Riley.

Laughter flickered through the blue of his eyes. Blushing, Morgan dumped all her packages on the other bed.

Mike said, ''I'm going to give you a shot for the pain, Riley, it'll probably put you out for a few hours—turn your back, Morgan.'' He then went on imperturbably, ''Stay off your leg as much as you can, don't drive for at least a week, and have it checked in a few days again. I've got to get back to the hospital now, but tomorrow I'll bring a picnic lunch here at noon and we'll eat on the patio. See you, Morgan. Cheers, buddy.''

With a quick wave he was gone. Riley remarked, ''He's been in a hurry as long as I've known him. We used to play handball and poker when we should have been studying.'' He yawned. ''You'd better get yourself something to eat, I'm out for the count.''

He'd showered, and he still hadn't offered to kiss her. She should have asked the lingerie store if her nightgown was returnable, Morgan thought unhappily, and watched as Riley's lashes fell to his cheeks. After she'd hidden her own package in a drawer, she went outside.

She visited the local museum, browsed in a bookstore, checked on Riley and found him dead asleep, and had a solitary, if extremely good, dinner in the restaurant. All her nerves on edge, she quietly opened the door to their room and stepped inside. Riley was still asleep.

She could leave him a note, take her car and go back to her campsite. The moon was full and she had a flashlight.

It would be the sensible thing to do. Her mother and father would applaud such a rational decision. As for Riley, she'd be willing to bet he wouldn't even realize she'd gone until tomorrow morning. Whatever Mike had given him had knocked him out.

The moonlight lay full on the bed, falling on Riley's bare chest and across his face. A strong face. A very masculine face. A face she had seen contorted with pain, torn by passion and alight with laughter.

She lowered the blinds and remembered how he had thrown all his weight on his bad leg to lift her out of reach of the rattlesnake. She remembered how he'd held her as she wept, and how they'd argued incessantly since they'd met. She remembered how his face had gentled when he'd described the ocean he loved.

It was her choice. She could turn her back on all this and walk out. And if she said in the note that she didn't want to see him again, she was almost certain he wouldn't come after her.

Or she could stay. And risk whatever might happen.

Risk that nothing might happen, she thought ironically, the way Riley's been behaving ever since real beds have become part of the scenery. Condoms or no condoms.

It was her choice. A choice, she sensed, whose results would affect her for the rest of her life whether she went or stayed.

Safety versus risk, that's what it came down to. Detachment versus the chance of intimacy. Solitude versus making love with a man of unknown depths and uncharted waters.

Her heart was pounding in her chest so loudly she was almost afraid it would wake him. He gave a small sigh, turned his cheek to the pillow, and lay still again.

His every movement filled her body with a wild longing.

Morgan opened the drawer in the bureau, took out the bag that contained the nightgown, and went into the bathroom. She soaked for a long time in a lather of bubble bath, dried herself, put on the nightgown and looked in the mirror.

A brilliant-eyed stranger looked back at her, her body limned by the clinging silk, her cleavage a shadowed valley, her hair like fire. Morgan tilted her chin. The decision was made. She was staying.

When she went back into the bedroom, she didn't even hesitate. First she put the array of little envelopes on the bedside table beside him. Then, as though she'd been doing it for years, she lifted the covers and slid into bed beside Riley. He was lying on his back. She curled into his side, put her arm over his ribs and her head on the pillow next to his. The pillowcase was also sage green. One of her favorite colours, she thought, and closed her eyes. Oddly, she felt neither afraid nor ravaged by desire. She simply felt peaceful.

She was where she needed and wanted to be. And that, for now, was enough.

Morgan woke to the sound of a man's voice and the touch of his hand. She blinked, because a soft golden light was shining right across the bed and for a moment she thought it was morning. Then Riley interposed his big body between her and the lamplight, and she saw the pools of darkness in the corners of the room, and saw, too, that his face was full of wonderment. "Morgan," he whispered, "beautiful Morgan...I was half afraid I'd wake up and find you gone."

She shifted a little, the better to see into the blue depths of his eyes. "I thought of leaving," she said honestly.

"But you didn't."

"I figured I'd regret it if I walked away from you. Riley, why didn't you kiss me after Mike left?"

"I didn't want to start something I knew I was in no shape to finish," he said promptly.

Something troubled her about this response, although she couldn't have said what. "I wondered if perhaps you'd changed your mind. That now we were back in civilization, you were having second thoughts."

"Not even the most fleeting of second thoughts." He smiled at her with infinite tenderness, brushing at the silk folds that lay over her breast. "I don't think this came out of your backpack."

"I bought it yesterday. To give me courage."

"Courage is integral to you, Morgan." As though he couldn't help himself Riley ran his hand across the swell of her breast, down the concavity of her belly to the slender length of her thigh, following all the curves of her body. Laying claim to her, she thought, and trembled to his touch.

He said huskily, "We've got the protection we need. So we can make love, dearest Morgan. If you want to."

Her choice had been made hours ago. "Oh, yes," she said, and smiled back.

"I want to leave the light on. So I can see you."

Shyness brought color to her cheeks. She ran one finger along his lower lip, her own lip caught between her teeth. "I want to see you, too." In sudden, fierce intensity she added, "Make love to me, Riley. Free me to take all the risks I've never taken before…risks I can't even imagine. Although since meeting you I know they exist. Please?"

He lifted the weight of her hair back from her face. "I'll do anything you want of me," he said, and lowered his head to kiss her.

As earlier Morgan had felt peaceful, it seemed now as though the urgency had gone from Riley, and with it any uncertainty. His kisses were deep and leisurely, his hands moved over the cool silk with an unhurried sensuality that spoke of abundant time. As he brushed her hair back from her face, dropping kisses over her eyelids, her cheekbones, the curve of her ears, he murmured, "Only one proviso. Should you get carried away by passion, don't kick my leg."

"I won't. Kick you, I mean." She gazed at him through her lashes and said provocatively, "Do you think I'll get carried away by passion?"

As he ran his tongue along her lower lip, he must have heard the tiny catch in her breath. "I'm going to do my best to ensure that you do."

In a rush she said, "All of a sudden I'm frightened."

Utterly serious, he said, "A canyon you've never walked."

"Is it a sea you've never sailed?"

"Of course. Why do you think I'm going so slow? Because I have the feeling we're heading smack-dab into a hurricane."

"*You're* frightened, too?"

"Sure am."

"I'm glad it's not just me," she announced, and reached up to run her fingers through his hair. It was springy and soft to the touch. "You don't know how often I've wanted to do that," she said with a satisfied smile.

He took her palm and pressed it to his chest, where she could feel the heavy strokes of his heart. Then he drew it lower down his body, watching her face change. As dark hair at his navel slid beneath her hand, she whispered, "You have the advantage of me. No clothes."

"Equality, huh?" he said, threw back the covers and began edging her gown slowly up over her knees. Again Morgan's breath caught in her throat. His naked body, strongly carved, fully aroused, was both beautiful to her and exciting beyond all her imaginings.

His hand was traveling the length of her leg. She shivered in violent anticipation, reached over and kissed him full on the mouth, her tongue dancing with his. The storm, she thought dimly, was building. And she was going to walk full into it.

Then she felt him touch the joining of her thighs. Another shudder rippled through her; instinctively she opened to him, pulling him down on top of her. His finger on the soft wet petals of her flesh became the center of her world; into this world she gathered her own explorations, the jut of Riley's hipbone, his taut buttocks, and, finally, the silken hardness of his own center.

Mine, she thought, caressing him with a sensuality that, for all its novelty, seemed utterly natural to her.

He groaned her name, abandoning any pretense that he was still at the storm's fringe as he roughly lifted her gown to bare the ivory planes of her belly and the rise of her breasts. She lifted her arms, saw him toss the gown behind her, and with a humility that touched her soul realized he was wonderstruck by her nudity. "It's only me," she faltered.

He looked right at her, his eyes like blue fire. "I never imagined you could be this beautiful."

In a small voice she said, "That's exactly the way I feel about you."

As though words were inadequate for his needs, Riley cupped her face in his palms and kissed her, an ardent, hungry kiss that streaked through her limbs with all the heat of the desert sun. She kissed him back, matching intimacy with intimacy, caress with caress, and somewhere at the very back of her brain wondered which she would die from first: pleasure or the driving ache of passion.

Then Riley rested the weight of her breasts in his

hands, lowered his head and kissed their tips, as hard as the small stones of the canyon floor. Morgan cried out his name in a broken voice, her features blurred by desire, and fell back on the mattress. Wanting only to feel his weight cover her, she drew him down on top of her, the taut wall of his chest abrading her softness. Her hips arched beneath him in ancient invitation. He gasped, "Wait, Morgan, wait..." and rolled over to get one of the small envelopes on the table beside him.

"I bought those and I forgot all about them," she said blankly.

He grinned at her, a grin of such carefree youthfulness that she was disarmed. "I'll take that as a compliment," he said.

"I think you'd be safe to do so."

With sudden intensity he said, "There are little flecks of gold in your eyes, why have I never noticed that before?"

"Riley," she chuckled, and moved her hips very suggestively again, "we've never been this close before." Clasping him by the shoulder, she added with a kind of impetuous naïveté, "I never realized that sex could have laughter in it. That one minute I can feel I'll absolutely die if you don't enter me, and the next I can be laughing at something you've just said." Her brow crinkled. "That's peculiar, isn't it?"

"Maybe," Riley said, giving her a smile whose tenderness caused something to shift, physically, within her, "it's called intimacy."

"Oh. I hadn't thought of that. But I didn't mean I wanted you to stop," she said, and blushed when he began to laugh again. "You're gorgeous all the time," she added, "but when you laugh...hey, you're irresistible."

"Gorgeous and irresistible, hmm?" he murmured, and with easy strength lifted her by the waist to straddle him.

The light kindled emerald sparks in her irises, shadowing the little hollow in her throat where her pulse bumped against her skin. He said, a note in his voice that was new to her, "Take me now, Morgan," and played with her breasts as she leaned over him, her mane of hair brushing his bare shoulders.

He slid into her as though she had been made for him, impaling her on a surge of such primitive hunger that laughter was banished. As the implacable rhythms claimed them both, she gazed right into his eyes, wanting him to see not only the nakedness of her body but also that of her soul: a far greater intimacy. Enmeshed in forces as old as time, she watched the storm gather in him, and felt it fling them both into the stillness that was its heart. Her sharp cry of completion echoed his harsher cry; gradually her throbbing body quietened, her pulses slowed.

With unconscious grace she collapsed on top of him, although even then she remembered to avoid his injured leg. As he kissed her, the sweetly scented mass of her hair enveloped him. He was hers, she thought possessively. Hers alone. "I want to stay here forever," she murmured, rubbing her cheek against his.

"Are you all right?"

"All right?" she repeated with a breathless giggle. "Devastated, delirious, replete, exhausted, peaceful and astounded...does that add up to all right?"

Riley took her chin in his lean fingers. "Are you trying to tell me that perhaps, just perhaps, you did see lightning?"

He wasn't joking. Her smile faded and sudden tears gleamed in her eyes. "Oh, Riley," she said helplessly, "it wasn't just lightning. The whole universe moved."

"It did for me, too," he said quietly. "Don't cry, Morgan, I hate to see you cry."

A tear plopped onto his cheek. "I'm so happy it frightens me," she whispered.

He wrapped his arms around her protectively. "You don't have to be frightened. Not if we're together."

But what if we're not? What then?

She didn't know where that voice had come from. Wherever it was, she didn't want to listen to it. Not now. Not when Riley was holding her as if she were the only woman in the world. With a small sigh Morgan rested her cheek on his shoulder. "Do you mind if I fall asleep?" she said fuzzily. And did.

CHAPTER SEVEN

MORGAN WOKE TO the sound of a man's voice singing lustily in the shower. Opera, she thought with a quiver of amusement. *Carmen*. That was certainly a stormy enough love affair. Although not, if she recalled rightly, one with a happy ending.

Why hadn't Riley woken her before he got up?

Perhaps, she thought, because they'd woken at dawn, and in the soft light filtering through the blinds had made love again, intensely, almost in silence, and to the same devastating climax.

She burrowed her face into the pillow, catching the scent of his body, stretching her own body luxuriously. She felt wonderful. She also felt as though she'd like to make love all over again. Right this minute. For the third time.

She'd never felt that way with Tomas, or with Chip. With them she'd felt kind of relieved it was over and that she could go back to being herself.

With Riley she became most truly herself.

The singing stopped along with the swish of water. Maybe, Morgan thought, she could entice Riley back to bed. It might be rather fun to try that.

A few moments later she heard him approach the bed. She said, opening one eye and allowing her voice a dramatic tremor worthy of Carmen, "I'm feeling sorry for myself. All alone in this big bed." With wicked swiftness she tweaked at the towel around his hips.

He sat down beside her, smoothing her hair. "Complaining already?"

She twisted in the bed so that she was lying naked

across his lap, gazing up at him soulfully. "Abandoned, that's me. Do you always sing opera in the shower?"

"I like the Nitty Gritty Dirt Band, too." He ran a lazy hand down her belly. "Do you know what the time is, Morgan?"

She made a wild guess. "Eight-thirty."

"Five past eleven. At noon Mike's coming for lunch. He's a very good friend, but I'm not sure I want him to discover me in the act of ravishing your gorgeous body, my darling."

"Five past *eleven*?" she squawked. "It can't be."

He consulted the clock radio by the bed. "Six minutes past, actually. We used up a fair bit of energy in the night. Or had you forgotten?"

She loved the way laughter lines crinkled at the corners of his eyes. She loved the way his mouth curved in a smile, too. She said, "If you get me started on last night, we'll never get out of here."

"So you'd like to make love again?"

"Only if the bookstore's closed," Morgan said impudently.

He bent and kissed her with a comprehensiveness that left her breathless. "Get dressed. Now."

"Kissing me like that," she puffed, "isn't the way to entice me out of bed, Riley Hanrahan."

"I'll make a note of it."

He stood up and stretched. Morgan watched the smooth slide of muscle and sinew lift his rib cage and said hastily, "How's your leg?"

"I'll have to tell Mike that making love is a surefire cure for bullet wounds," he said. "They should add it to all the medical books. Now, where are these clothes you bought me?"

Morgan got up as he dropped the towel. His back was to her, with its long indentation of spine. In sudden and inexplicable fright she heard herself say, "Riley, you won't just disappear, will you?"

He turned, frowning at her. "Where did that come from?"

"I—I don't know," she stammered. "Ignore it, please."

"I won't disappear, Morgan. Not unless you want me to. And maybe not even then without a struggle." He was still frowning. "Get dressed and we'll go for a coffee."

Fifteen minutes later they walked to the restaurant. Riley looked extremely handsome in the cords and deep blue shirt Morgan had picked out for him. Discovering they were too hungry to wait for Mike, they ordered juice and muffins and started on coffee. Stirring in sugar, Riley said soberly, "Tell me something, Morgan. This is October. Why aren't you in school?"

Very precisely she put her cup down on its saucer. It was an obvious question. So why hadn't she seen it coming? "My reasons are personal," she said, and because he'd taken her by surprise she sounded distant and unfeeling.

A muscle twitched in his jaw. "Most reasons are."

"Here comes our juice," she said with a false smile.

Once the waitress was out of earshot, Riley said, "So tell me your reasons."

"I don't want to talk about it."

He stayed her hand as she reached for her orange juice. "What we did in bed last night felt pretty personal to me."

Her chin lifted to match his anger. "That was sex. This is different."

"So in between bouts of lovemaking you plan to talk about the weather and the world news? No dice, Morgan."

"This is a public place and we're fighting again," she said coldly, and tossed back her juice.

"I won't compromise on this one. What happened last night changed me. *You've* changed me. But if you're not prepared to be intimate out of bed as well as in it, then tonight we'll sleep in separate rooms."

She felt as if he'd stabbed her with his knife. "Compromise is the only way people manage to have relationships and how dare you give me an ultimatum like that!"

"Very easily," he said in a hard voice. "Because I mean every word of it."

"You're the one who didn't want to get involved!"

"I am involved. Whether I want to be or not."

"My parents never in their life fought like you and I do."

"Then it must have been an exceedingly shallow marriage."

The waitress put a basket of warm muffins on the table, along with butter, jam and marmalade. Morgan looked at all this in dismay, wondering how on earth she was going to swallow even one bite. "I do not have to answer a single one of your questions," she said, and recklessly slathered butter over a banana muffin.

For a moment she thought Riley was going to push back his chair and leave. As she chewed a mouthful that might just as well have been made of cardboard, she watched him battle down his anger, his fingertips white where they gripped the edge of the table. "Look," he said hoarsely, "I'm new to the game called intimacy and I'm not handling this very well. You asked me why I didn't kiss you yesterday after Mike left. It was because I was equating kissing with sex and I knew I was in no shape to take you to bed right then. But when we made love last night, I learned something very basic. Kissing can sometimes be about sex, of course it can. But it's always about intimacy.'' He paused, staring at the muffin on his plate as if he wasn't quite sure what it was. ''Morgan, you can't share your body with me and not the rest of your life.''

Her own anger fled, for there was genuine pain in his face. This matters to him, she thought. A lot. So I must matter to him. All of me, not just my body. ''I'm new to it, too,'' she muttered and watched jam drip from a soggy piece of muffin.

''Ever since we've met I thought you looked tired. Deep down tired, not the kind a good night's sleep gets rid of. But that's not something you say to a woman you're trying to impress…gee, Morgan, you sure look tired today. So I kept quiet about it.''

She looked up. ''I'm on leave. Burnout.'' She scowled ferociously. ''It sounds so damned trite. The in-word. Half the country's suffering from it.''

''Including you.''

Her shoulders slumped. ''Mmm…including me.''

''Tell me about your job. You teach in Boston, is that what you told me? High school or junior high?''

Uneasily at first she began to talk about her school, until the words started tripping from her tongue. Overcrowding, drugs, knifings, prostitution, hunger, racism, she spilled it all out. And underlying every word, without her knowing it, ran both her love for her students and her job, and her deep frustration at impediments that were too often insurmountable.

Eventually she stopped, staring at her now-cold muffin in revulsion, feeling tiredness settle like stone griffins on her shoulders. Riley said gently, ''How long have you been in that school?''

''Seven years. Ever since I graduated.''

''Morgan, seven years in an environment like that would kill a horse. You don't have to feel ashamed that you're exhausted.''

She gaped at him. "How did you know that I'm ashamed?"

"Why else wouldn't you tell me about it?"

She sighed. "You're right, of course. Even now I feel guilty. I should be in school instead of camping in the desert."

"When do you have to go back?"

"After Christmas."

Absently he played with the handle on his cup. "When you found me in the canyon, I really threw a monkey wrench into your life, didn't I?"

"Sort of," she said with a tiny smile.

"So where do we go from here?" he said heavily.

He had asked the one question to which she had no answer. "My whole upbringing tells me to head back to the ledge. Today. By myself."

"Is that what you're going to do?"

"That's hardly a fair question!"

"It's the only question that matters."

He signaled to the waitress to refill his coffee. As he stirred in sugar, Morgan said at random, "You have one heck of a sweet tooth."

He grinned. "The nuns didn't go in for frills like sugar. I've been making up for it ever since."

"They no doubt were very good to you," she said, knowing she was verbalizing an important truth, "but you couldn't have learned much about intimacy in an orphanage."

"I loved Sister Anna. But she had seventy other kids to love besides me. You're the one who's shown me what I've been missing all my life. In less than a week. I told you you'd turned my world upside down and if I'm behaving less than perfectly it's because I'm still reeling from shock."

"You seem to have it all figured out," she said with a touch of desperation. "I wish I did."

"Hell, Morgan, if I'm giving you the impression I've got everything under control, I'm a damn good actor." He took a big gulp of coffee. "I asked you where we go from here. I know where I want us to go. Both of us. To Salt Lake City."

"What for?" she asked bluntly.

"I've got an appointment there the day after tomorrow. Concerning Beth's will. And I don't want to leave you here."

Even though she knew that sooner or later they'd have to talk about Beth, she didn't want to right now. Because Beth was just one more complication. Instead Morgan said the obvious. "Salt Lake City isn't the desert."

"You've got until Christmas."

"It snows in the desert, Riley. I'm not equipped for winter camping. Which," she added wildly, "isn't the issue, I know it's not, and shouldn't we be going back to the room?"

He said harshly, "It's my turn now. *You* won't just disappear, Morgan, will you?"

She pushed her plate away. "If I'm going to leave you, I'll let you know."

Plainly he had been looking for a different answer. She stood up. "I hope I'm more interested in Mike's picnic than I was in those muffins. Let's go."

Mike's idea of a picnic was so palatial that Morgan recovered her appetite. She ate heartily, laughed a lot and was crushingly polite to Riley. She also, inadvertently, learned considerably more about him. Mike asked a lot of questions and eventually Riley started talking about his work. He described the songs of the humpbacks, the mothering skills of right whales and his few sightings of the rare blue whale, and all the while his passionate love for these great mammals of the ocean, so mysterious and so threatened, shone unguardedly in his face.

By the time he'd finished, Morgan had a lump in her throat. She also found herself with a strong desire to go with him on one of his expeditions and see for herself the leap of dolphins around the bow or the smooth rise from the waves of a finback's brown bulk. All her spare time in the last few years had been spent in the desert. There were other worlds to explore, she thought; and felt her mind leap to the world she had explored in the night, the world of Riley's body.

Terrified that her thoughts would show on her face, she loaded her fork with the most delicious key lime pie she'd ever eaten and said enthusiastically, "You must tell us where you got this, Mike, it's scrumptious."

Mike looked a little surprised by her change of subject; but he was an agreeable man, and the conversation switched from whales to culinary matters. At one-twenty, after gathering up the remains of the picnic, Mike took his leave. "Appointments all afternoon. 'Bye, Morgan, it was good to meet you." He clapped Riley on the shoulder. "Good luck in the big city, fella. And look after that leg. See you in January if not before."

Riley limped out to the car with him. Morgan stayed where she was. She had no idea what she was going to do for the rest of the afternoon. Or for the rest of her life.

Riley's plan had been accomplished. They'd made love. Now what?

From the patio door Riley said, "I've got to put my leg up, Morgan. Keep me company?"

She stood up and went inside. Fiddling with the catch on the door, she said, "I like your friend Mike."

"One of the best." With a muffled grunt Riley hauled his leg up on the bed. "I've got to tell you about Beth, Morgan. It's not fair to keep you wondering."

She gave him a bright, insincere smile. "Well, it's not really any of my business, is it?"

"Will you for Pete's sake stop acting as though I'm a total stranger?" he roared. "The whole time Mike was here you behaved like my maiden aunt. You're my lover, Morgan. My lover! D'you hear me?"

"I'm sure they can hear you at the front desk," she said spiritedly. "How else was I supposed to behave? Would you rather I'd worn a black bra and nibbled on your ear?"

As abruptly as he'd lost his temper, Riley began to laugh, great hoots of laughter from deep in his chest. "Yeah," he gasped, "I'd have liked that just fine. Do you *own* any black bras?"

"I do not!"

"We'll have to remedy that. Come here, Morgan Cassidy. Now."

It was on the tip of her tongue to say, Come and get me. Which would be a very immature way to speak to a man with a sore leg. She sat down on the opposite side of the bed, presenting him with her profile, her nose in the air. "I don't—"

And then she said nothing more for the simple reason that Riley had lunged across the bed, had caught her in his arms and was kissing her with an incendiary combination of rage and desire. She could have struggled. Instead she kissed him back as though it had been months rather than hours since they had lain together in this very bed, months in which she had thought of nothing else but her longing to make love to him. Her fingers fumbled with the buttons on his new blue shirt, tangled themselves in his body hair, then clasped his bare shoulders.

He hauled the waist of her shirt from her trousers, and tossed his own shirt to the carpet. It took longer to rid him of his new cords, which then joined her bush pants at the foot of the bed along with their socks. Flesh to flesh, they kissed, stroked and kissed again in a crescendo of passion that was wordless and fierce and all-consuming. As he thrust his way into her warmth and wetness, Morgan heard him say her name over and over again, like a litany.

"Sweetheart, sweetheart," she pleaded, "now, oh now, please," and wrapped her legs around him as his body pulsed to its release and her own rose to meet him, flinging her past a rainbow of colors into the velvet darkness that was satiation.

She was trembling lightly all over. Riley lifted his weight onto his elbows, his big body covering her like a shield. His breath was rasping in his throat, and she could feel against her ribs the rapid thud of his heartbeat. She reached up to smooth his hair back from his forehead, and managed a saucy grin. "How did that happen?"

"You seduced me," he said, trapping her fingers in his and kissing them, one by one.

She snorted. "You can move like greased lightning when you choose to, Riley Hanrahan."

"Got to supply you with lightning somehow."

"There's no energy shortage when you're around," she said warmly. "And if I ever seduce you, I trust it will take a little longer than ten seconds."

"That could be our next move," he said hopefully, sliding his lips across her palm.

She said in her most schoolmarmish voice, "You'll have to wait five minutes."

"Then I've got a question. Did you call me sweetheart? In the heat of the moment?"

Her cheeks, already warm, flushed scarlet. "I never use words like that, I don't know what came over me."

"Good," he said.

I could get used to this, Morgan thought faintly. To the laughter lines around Riley's eyes; to the scent of his skin, so unmistakably his, so engraved on my own; to the joining of our bodies in passion and delight.

For once, the solitude of her tent in the desert did not appeal. How could she let Riley leave for Salt Lake City tomorrow without her?

I'm losing my independence, she thought, panic-stricken. What if I get so I need him? Then I'll never get away.

"What's wrong, Morgan?"

Intimacy or no intimacy, she wasn't ready to share her feelings with him. She said, pulling back a little, "You said you were going to tell me about Beth."

"Dammit, yes," he said restively. He pulled himself further up on the pillow so he could look down into her face. "There's not a whole lot to tell you. I have no idea why I should be mentioned in her will, or why Mr. Atherton—he's her lawyer—is making such a fuss because I'm so late getting there. He's as closemouthed as a clam, that man."

Out of the blue Morgan was aware that she was afraid. She pulled the covers up, needing something to do, and heard him say, "She died a month ago in hospital. A routine check turned up a particularly virulent form of cancer and she only lived three weeks." He rubbed at his forehead. "She and I haven't been in touch for seven or eight years, she made it clear when we parted that she didn't want any further contact between us. Which is why this whole business with the will is so strange."

Morgan's blithe theory about an elderly philanthropist was becoming more and more unlikely. Dry-mouthed, she said, "How did you meet her?"

"In California. I was there researching migration routes of gray whales and she'd been touring the vineyards. We met in San Diego, quite by chance." He broke off. "Hell, Morgan, I hate telling you all this."

She hated hearing it. "Go on," she said.

"She was very forthright. She wanted an affair for as long as we were in California, but no commitment beyond that. I never saw her home in Utah, she never saw mine in Maine. That was fine with me. I wasn't into commitment." Absently he played with Morgan's hair, his mind obviously elsewhere. "So for a month we were together. She was pretty, and good company, and never minded when I had to go to sea. I wasn't in love with her, nor she, I'm sure, with me. When she went back to Utah—we didn't even exchange addresses—I missed her for a while. But then I was offered a bunk for two months on a research vessel, so I forgot about her." He ran his fingers through his hair. "Until Mr. Atherton phoned, all in a dither that I wouldn't drop everything and fly out to Salt Lake City that very day."

Morgan lay still. It was one thing for Riley to have told her about calm and serene women in the abstract. It was quite another to have the name and description of a particular woman, one to whom he had meant enough that she had left him something in her will.

How could she, Morgan, be jealous of a dead woman? A woman, moreover, who had died tragically young?

Unconsciously she moved further away from him in the bed, and when he reached out one hand to take her by the shoulder, she shrank from him. He said, "I'm thirty-five years old, Morgan. I come with a past. And I was never in love with her."

"I just wish you'd told me sooner!"

"How could I? If you and I weren't going to be together, why would I tell you? And once we'd become lovers, it was too late."

Morgan wasn't in the mood for logical explanations. She said raggedly, "I'm going to have a shower and go for a walk."

His fingers dug into her flesh. "But you're coming back."

"I said I wouldn't leave without telling you. I've got to think, Riley, I'm all confused and upset."

He said flatly, "I want you to go with me tomorrow. You're important to me. In a way Beth never was. I can't explain that or justify it. You just have to take it on trust."

"Was she calm and serene?" Morgan blurted.

"Yes," he said with a wayward glint of laughter. "Not a bit like you."

"I am not normally a woman who swears a lot. But right now," Morgan said tightly, "if I had a dictionary that was nothing but cusswords I'd begin at A and I wouldn't stop until I reached Z."

Straight-faced, Riley said, "The Cassidy version of 'Sesame Street.'"

She was plucking her scattered garments from the bed and the carpet, loftily ignoring both her nudity and his teasing. "Go to sleep," she ordered. "I'll be back in time for supper. Maybe by then I'll have some inkling of what I'm going to do with my life."

Riley, wisely, said nothing. Morgan slammed the bathroom door and locked it and glared at her reflection in the mirror. It didn't really seem very likely that a shower and a walk could sort out her confusion. It would take a miracle to do that. She grabbed the plastic shower cap, made a futile effort to stuff her springy curls into it, and turned on the tap.

Morgan was quite right. The walk did nothing to clarify her tangled emotions. In fact, if anything, it added to them, because she found herself standing outside the lingerie boutique with a strong desire to go in and buy a black bra. Riley would like that.

Morosely she crossed the street and bought a cappuccino in the little coffee shop. Riley would also like her to go to Salt Lake City. Is that what she was going to do? To please him?

Or was she going to do it to please herself?

The chocolate sprinkles were melting into the white foam. Just like she melted every time he even looked at her. Let alone smiled at her. Or kissed her.

She wanted very badly to believe that what was between her and Riley was only sex. Sex was definitely part of it, Morgan thought, burying her face in her coffee cup. But this mysterious word intimacy that they kept bandying about was beginning to seem as important as sex, yet inextricable from it. *Did* her parents know about that kind of intimacy? Although she'd never doubted the strong current of affection between them, they hadn't been a demonstrative couple, and they'd certainly never yelled at each other the way she and Riley did with exhilarating frequency.

Because Riley made her feel alive. Morgan knew that. Distressingly alive, at times. Deliriously alive at others. But unquestionably and vibrantly alive.

Salt Lake City, here I come. She drained her cup, left a tip and went across the street. By the time she came out of the boutique, she had spent rather a lot of money. But black, she thought immodestly, had always looked good on her.

She wandered further along the street, went into another boutique and came out with a delightful dress in soft blue denim with a demure black velvet collar and cuffs, and a gorgeously shiny full-length black raincoat. As she headed for the shoe shop, she realized it was ages since she'd spent money on her wardrobe; in school she tended to wear jeans and sweatshirts, like her students. Ten minutes later a pair of slim black leather boots had joined her purchases. She then found some dangly black earrings in a jeweler's, and bought makeup and a black velvet bow for her hair in a drugstore.

Three cheers for credit cards, she thought, and walked back to the motel.

Riley had just come out of the bathroom; he was wearing his cords, his hair clinging wetly to his scalp and a towel draped over his arm. As his eyes flew to her face, Morgan realized something else: Riley wasn't as confident of her as he might like to appear. She said lightly, tossing her bags on the other bed, "I bought some clothes. So I wouldn't disgrace you in Salt Lake City."

He let out his breath in a little hiss. "Will you model them for me?"

"Not today. But tomorrow evening you're going to take me out for dinner." She smiled at him complacently. "You'll like what I bought."

"In that case," he said, "we'd better go to the police station and persuade them to give me back my luggage. In honor of Mr. Atherton, I packed my best suit."

She remembered the black underwear and blushed. "Let's get it over with, I didn't care for that policeman. And, Riley, I'm getting up early tomorrow morning, and I'm hiking into the campsite to bring back my gear."

She had half expected him to argue. "That makes sense," he said. "I don't think Howard and Dez are anywhere in the area by now. The police impounding my car would have made them hightail it out of here."

"You trust me to come back?"

"Yes. You'd tell me if you weren't going to, because you're honest." He scrubbed at his hair with the towel. "Honesty is one of those virtues that rarely gets mentioned in steamy love stories. But for me, it's basic. And you've got it."

"You, too," she said humbly.

He grinned at her. "You're also argumentative, unpredictable and extremely sexy."

"You, too." Batting her lashes, she dodged as he

reached out for her. ''Police station, Riley. Sex after that.''

''I could change your mind,'' he growled.

''Yep.''

He flicked her bottom with the corner of the towel and put on his shirt. Morgan, humming under her breath, put her purchases in the closet and knew herself to be happy.

CHAPTER EIGHT

BY NOON the next day Morgan and Riley were heading north on the first leg of their journey. Her gear was stashed in the trunk; she was wearing her bush pants and boots. Her campsite, rather to her surprise, had caused her no second thoughts. For now, she wanted to be with Riley rather than camping alone in the desert. And that was that.

They were driving toward the interstate when Riley said, "Now's a good time for you to tell me about Chip."

Morgan had been admiring the smooth expanse of grasslands and the distant, cloud-capped mountain range. "I don't want to," she said. "How's that for honesty?"

He rested his palm on her thigh. "Come clean, Morgan. You didn't want to tell me about burnout, either."

"You're like a dentist, always prodding and poking," she said crossly. "Oh, look, there's a red-tailed hawk."

Riley's eyes didn't leave her face. "Dentists add to the beauty of your smile. What's his last name and how old is he?"

Morgan had never really sorted out what Chip had meant to her. Instead, in the last year, she'd retreated into herself and increased her workload. Which, more or less directly, had led her to Riley.

"Chip Palermo, thirty-one, low-key kind of guy, teacher at my school, collects antique glass, known him for seven years."

She stopped abruptly. "Keep going," said Riley.

She frowned at the long ribbon of highway. "Dated

him, on and off, for four years. We were friends. Buddies. Went to movies. Ate pizza. Jogged together in the park. Worked together with the kids after school in athletics and drama. It was so reliable and easygoing, and just what I needed—it helped me keep the lid on all the problems at school.''

''What happened?''

Morgan sighed. ''A year ago September on my twenty-eighth birthday we went out for dinner. We drank too much wine and ended up in bed. We'd never done that, you see, it hadn't been an issue. And it ruined everything. The whole friendship got strained and awkward and horrible, and we started avoiding each other. Then the first thing you know he falls in love with the new art teacher and all last spring they have this scorching affair right under my nose...they're getting married next month.''

''I see,'' said Riley thoughtfully. ''Chip and you sound rather like your parents' marriage. No ups and downs.''

''Except that sex wrecked the relationship.''

''Is he another reason you're so tired?''

''Oh, well, there was Sally, too—I might as well give you my whole life story while I'm at it. Sally's my best friend. She got bronchitis at the end of term, when we're all zombies anyway, and over the summer it turned into pneumonia. So I spent most of August and September looking after her and her four cats.'' She gave him a rueful smile. ''I don't care if I ever see kitty litter again.''

''You know what I'd like to do?'' Riley said with sudden violence. ''I'd like to spirit you to a Caribbean island and keep you there for at least six months. Doing absolutely nothing.''

It sounded like heaven. ''I don't feel tired when I'm with you,'' Morgan confessed in a small voice.

e're getting in deeper and deeper all the
.you know that, don't you?''

s hand felt heavy on her leg and the same violence
had roughened his voice. ''Scary,'' she said.

''Yeah…maybe for once we should talk about the
weather. For instance, it looks like we're heading into
rain.''

''We should soon reach the interstate,'' Morgan said,
and grimaced as they passed a dead coyote on the shoulder of the road.

The interstate was four-lane, the rain held off, and
they talked of nothing but inconsequentials. They passed
through the brown haze over the steel plants in Provo
and Orem, and a little later pulled off for coffee so Riley
could stretch his legs. By five they were booked into a
hotel in Salt Lake City.

Morgan was beginning to regret her spending spree of
the day before. Riley didn't look in the mood for black
underwear; he'd withdrawn from her in a way she didn't
like at all. With a touch of desperation she said, ''What's
wrong, Riley?''

He was shaking out his suit. ''I'll be glad when this
thing with Atherton is dealt with,'' he said tersely. ''I've
got a bad feeling about it. Must be the Irish in me.''

''Oh. So it's nothing to do with me?''

''Of course not,'' he said in faint surprise. ''But I've
got the same kind of lump in my gut as when I'm swim-
ming too close to a whale fifty times my size in order
to free it from a fishing net. One flip of the tail and I'm
a goner.'' He hung his suit jacket on a wooden hanger.
''Morgan, will you go with me tomorrow? I know it's
a lot to ask. But I'd feel better if you were there.''

He needed her. That was what he was saying. She
said, ''Yes, I'll go.''

Lightly he rested his hands on her shoulders.
''Thanks.''

She would do a great deal more than beard the taciturn Mr. Atherton to bring that look to Riley's eyes. He added, dropping a kiss on the tip of her nose, "You did all the driving today. Why don't you soak in the tub while I go down to get a newspaper? Maybe there's a concert or a play you'd like to go to tonight."

"Okay," she said.

But Morgan didn't soak in the tub. She had a very quick shower instead. When Riley unlocked the door to their room, she was lying in a provocative pose on the sheets, clad in lacy black underwear complete with a minimalist bra and long black stockings, her hair a vivid cloud around her face.

He pulled the door shut and slid the chain in place, his blue eyes sparked with fire. "You've got a choice," he said. "Tickets for a ballet. Or me."

She gave him a sultry smile and moved her hips suggestively. "I did promise to seduce you."

He dropped the newspaper and hauled his shirt out of his waistband. "So you did. I'm glad you're a woman who keeps her promises."

He undressed in total silence. Then, naked and aroused, he walked toward the bed. And Morgan forgot all her preplanned moves and simply opened her arms to him.

Nine o'clock the next morning found Riley and Morgan standing outside the double mahogany doors that announced in polished brass letters the firm of Atherton, Williams and Atherton. Riley looked exceedingly handsome in his gray pinstripe suit and Morgan felt her best in her new dress and boots. Mr. Atherton didn't have to know she was wearing black underwear, she thought, and gave Riley's hand an encouraging squeeze.

He glanced down at her. "Have I told you yet this morning that you look very beautiful?" he said huskily, and in his face was all the memory of their lovemaking last night and of dinner eaten in bed because neither of them wanted to go out.

Some of her nervousness vanished. "You're the handsomest man in the state of Utah," she said pertly, her heart in her smile. "Also the sexiest."

"Don't feel you have to research Utah's male population to back up that last statement," he growled and lifted her hair to kiss her ear. Then he opened the door.

Wilfred Atherton was younger and more affable than Morgan had expected from Riley's comments. Riley introduced her as his friend and said in a tone that brooked no argument, "I want Miss Cassidy to be present, Mr. Atherton."

"Certainly," the lawyer said, aligning the file precisely with the corners of the leather blotter on top of his desk. He had thin fair hair and light blue eyes, and looked not altogether at his ease. Morgan felt her nerves tighten.

Wilfred Atherton cleared his throat, opened the file and passed Riley a letter. "I believe the most direct way to deal with this matter is to give you this letter," he said. "I have been apprised of its contents, although I was not permitted to divulge them until we were face-to-face. Perhaps you would read it, Mr. Hanrahan?"

Only Morgan, who was beginning to know Riley rather well, saw the tension in his jaw as he tore the envelope open and spread out the two sheets it contained. He started to read.

She watched the color drain from his face and heard the expensive notepaper crackle in his fingers as he gripped it more and more tightly. Her pulse began to race; her throat closed uncomfortably.

He read the letter through. Then, as though he couldn't believe the evidence of his own eyes, he read it again. Only then did he drop it on the desk and croak, "Is this *true*?"

"Absolutely, Mr. Hanrahan."

"God in heaven," said Riley.

"I can see that it must come as a surprise to you," Mr. Atherton said. "Perhaps when—"

"A surprise?" Riley snarled. "I've just discovered that I've got a seven-year-old daughter, and you talk about *surprise*?"

Morgan's gasp of shock brought his head around. He was white-faced, his eyes blank; not even in his worst moments in the desert had she seen him look so terrible. He said hoarsely, "You'd better read it, too, Morgan," and thrust the letter at her.

She swallowed hard, glanced at the signature at the end and began to read. The script was very neat, written in fountain pen on heavy vellum; the letter was dated seven years ago. Its gist was that Beth Slater had deliberately deceived Riley. She had wanted a child but not a husband; her month-long affair with Riley had achieved her aim. She did not once apologize for the deception. "I hope you never receive this letter," Morgan read, "because if you do it means I shall be dead. But should that happen, I'm giving my daughter into your custody as the biological father. One of the reasons I agreed to our affair was that I felt you were a man of intelligence and integrity who would make a good father should anything happen to me."

The words blurred in front of Morgan's eyes. Riley had a child. A daughter born seven years ago.

Terrified out of her wits, she threw the letter on the desk as though it were the deadliest of rattlesnakes.

Mr. Atherton ran his finger around his collar. "Miss Slater has been my client for many years. She drew up a new will when her daughter was born, and that document remains in effect now. In brief, she leaves her house to her brother; it's a very substantial house. The remainder of her estate—'' he mentioned a sum that made Morgan blink ''—she leaves to you, Mr. Hanrahan, for the care and support of your daughter. She wishes her brother to have no further dealings with the child. I'm sure you'd like to look over the will.''

The document he held out to Riley was bound in shiny dark green paper. Riley shook his head; he still looked like a man in shock. ''I'll take your word for it,'' he said.

''I had my secretary xerox a copy, you can take it with you.''

There was a silence. Then Riley, who had been gazing at the floor, looked up. ''What's her name?'' he said. ''My daughter's name?''

''Jennifer Elizabeth. She goes by Jenny.'' Mr. Atherton cleared his throat. ''I wouldn't presume to tell you what to do, Mr. Atherton. But Jenny should be in school, and I would hope that you'll take her to your home as soon as possible and get her settled. You live in Maine, do you not?''

''You mean she's not in school now? But if she's seven—''

The lawyer said delicately, ''Miss Slater preferred private tutoring. Entirely legal, of course,'' he finished hastily.

Riley leaned forward. ''What are you trying to tell me?''

''I'm sure when you meet Jenny, you'll come to your own conclusions,'' Mr. Atherton said, and made a little steeple of his fingers.

''I'm walking into this blind,'' Riley exploded. ''I need all the help I can get and I don't appreciate you holding back any information that might be of use.''

The lawyer glanced at the framed photo on his desk of an attractive blond woman with two little girls. Then he looked back at Riley. "I'm a father myself," he said, rather obviously. "If I were to give you any advice—strictly off the record, of course—I'd say take Jenny out of that house just as quickly as you can. Today wouldn't be too soon. She needs to go to a regular school and wear blue jeans and get dirty. And that, Mr. Hanrahan, is all you're getting out of me. Other than to say that I'm available to smooth out the legalities and financial transfers, and to explain any clauses of the will should you require me to do so. I would also appreciate it if you'd notify me when you plan to leave the state."

He passed Riley a hand-sketched map. "I took the liberty of showing you how to get to the house, it's a twenty-minute drive from the city."

Riley took the map and the plain brown envelope that contained the copy of the will. Gazing at the map as though it might blow up in his face, he pushed himself to his feet. "Thank you, Mr. Atherton, I'll be in touch. We're staying at the Wasatch Hotel if you need me."

All the way down on the elevator Riley stared stonily at the control panel. They walked out onto the street, into October sunshine and the roar of traffic. When they reached the car, he said abruptly, "I've got to be by myself for a few minutes, Morgan. Why don't I walk back to the hotel and you meet me there?"

"But—"

"If it's too far, I'll get a cab," he said curtly, and set off down the street as though demons were after him. He was, Morgan noticed with a catch at her heart, masking his limp as best he could. His hands were thrust in his pockets, his shoulders hunched.

Riley had a seven-year-old daughter. Named Jenny. Who was now in his sole custody. And who would be going with him to Maine very soon.

Which certainly changed things between herself and Riley. Altered them totally. It was one thing to embark on an affair with an unattached man, quite another to continue that affair when she'd just discovered the man in question was responsible for the upbringing of a small child. That in the next few days he'd be leaving for the other side of the country with that child.

Her heart felt like it was encased in lead, her throat as though it were encircled by a choke chain. But she couldn't just sit here. Hoping the problem would go away.

Morgan started the car and leaped away from the curb, passing Riley without acknowledging his presence, and driving to the hotel as fast as she could. There was a parking meter free right by the hotel. She pulled in and turned off the engine. A bus zipped past, followed by a police cruiser.

What had that policeman said, the one she'd disliked so much back in Sorel? If Riley had been left a million bucks, he'd said, it would be a motive for murder.

Beth's estate wasn't quite that much. But it was near. Which to Morgan seemed like a huge sum of money.

Perhaps Howard and Dez had been hired to get rid of Riley so the money would go to the unknown brother. If they'd been able to track Riley down in Sorel, it was entirely possible they knew where he was right now. And would try again.

Her palms were sweating. Morgan rubbed them on her new dress and tried to calm down. She'd been reading too many mysteries. Not even Dez with his minimal intelligence would shoot Riley down in the middle of the city.

They could run him down when he crossed the street. He wouldn't be able to jump out of the way because of his bad leg.

With a whimper of fear Morgan got out of the car. Riley would come that way, she thought, and started running along the sidewalk, scanning both sides of the road for his dark head. When she came to an intersection she turned right, thrusting her way through pedestrians with scant regard for good manners or for the toes of her new boots.

Five minutes later she was still running. Her imagination was also running, running away with her. What if Howard had posed as a cabdriver? She'd never see Riley again. She couldn't bear that. Her breath sobbing in her throat, she sprinted along the sidewalk.

And then she saw him. He was on the opposite side of the road, waiting for the light to change. She looked both ways and darted across the street, crying his name, ignoring the cabdriver who was racing the light and leaning on his horn. Riley grabbed her by the sleeve. "What the hell are you doing?"

She collapsed against him, gasping for breath. "You're s-safe," she sputtered.

"Of course I am." He pulled her out of the crosswalk, giving some curious bystanders a ferocious scowl. "Morgan, I'm quite capable of walking six blocks and I told you I wanted to be alone."

She stammered out her theory, which didn't sound very convincing now that she had her arms cinched around his waist. "So I c-came looking for you."

"Where's your car?"

"At the hotel."

He hailed a cab, thrust her in the back seat and got in beside her. He didn't look at all grateful for being rescued, she thought resentfully, and pulled her skirt down over her knees. Her boots, elegant though they were, had not been designed for running. "Next time I'll let you be the victim of a hit-and-run," she said meanly.

Riley said nothing. The cabbie pulled up by the hotel and Morgan climbed out, stalking back to her car. A parking ticket was flapping under her windshield wiper; she'd forgotten to put any money in the meter. She got in the car, slammed the door and flung the ticket in the back seat. As Riley climbed in, she said coldly, "Now what do you want to do?"

"I want to wake up," he said with savage emphasis. "Wake up and find out this is all a bad dream." He ran his fingers through his hair. "Let's go straight to the house."

"I'm not going. You can take a taxi."

His head swung around. "Look, it was nice of you to come running after me like that even if it wasn't necessary, and I'm sorry I'm in such a lousy mood. I want you to come with me."

Morgan hated the word nice, especially when it was used of her. "Jenny's your child, Riley. Not mine."

"You've got that wrong. She's Beth's child."

"You fathered her."

Violently he slammed his fist on the dash. "How could she have deceived me like that?" he blazed. "Deliberately. In cold blood. And then walk away as though nothing had happened. She never let me know she was pregnant. Never told me when my child was born. I still wouldn't know if she hadn't died. She didn't even apologize in the letter…how could she have behaved that way?"

He was haggard, his eyes burning in their sockets. Morgan hardened her heart. "How do I know? You're the one who knew her."

"I didn't know her at all! Because that's the other thing. I was utterly taken in. Here's this pleasant, serene woman who wants an affair with no commitments, right up your alley, Hanrahan, go for it." Bitterly he added, "I was thinking with my hormones, not my brain cells."

He was glaring at Morgan in a way that seared her to the soul. She spat, "Don't you dare look at me like that! I'm not Beth Slater."

As he rubbed at his forehead, Morgan watched reason

return to his eyes. "Sorry," he muttered. "I know you're not, of course I do. But I've been half crazy ever since I read that letter."

"I can understand why, don't think I'm being utterly unfeeling. But I still think you should take a cab."

He took a deep, slow breath. "Let's start over. Why don't you want to come with me?"

If he'd been half crazy, she'd been in a total panic ever since she'd read Beth's neat script with its devastating message. Panic so all-consuming she couldn't think straight. Which was one reason she'd gone running after him. Now, trusting her gut instincts, Morgan said, "You've got to make your own relationship with Jenny. She's *your* child. Yours and Beth's. My presence would just confuse the issue."

"Morgan," Riley said, "I don't know the first thing about kids. I haven't been with a seven-year-old since I was in the orphanage."

"Then you'd better start learning. Fast. I can't help you with that, Riley—it's your job."

"So what are you going to do? Head for the desert in your jazzy blue dress?"

"I don't *know*!"

"Start the goddamned car and let's get out there."

"You've got to think of Jenny," she stormed. "You and I aren't married or engaged or even in love, and—"

"I wouldn't be too sure about that," Riley said grimly.

"About what?" Morgan said, all her senses suddenly alert.

"I told you you've turned my world upside down. That I've been intimate with you in ways that are utterly new to me and that I want you both in bed and out. I don't know what being in love means, Morgan, it's new territory for me. But I figure what I've just told you might turn out to be one definition."

"I don't want you falling in love with me!"

"I haven't said I am," he grated. "Although if I were, would that be so terrible?"

"You're not the right man for me. You're nothing like the kind of man I've always known I'll marry."

"No, Chip was," he said acerbically. "Morgan, this is scarcely the time to discuss your prospective life part-ner—I do happen to have other things on my mind. Will you for Pete's sake start driving? We need Route 81 north."

He looked every bit as furious as she. And let's face it, Morgan, she thought turbulently, you know darn well you can't push him out of your car and drive away to the desert and never know what happened. You're in too deep for that.

If she were to be completely honest, she was also very curious to see Beth Slater's house. And to meet Jenny. Even though the prospect of that meeting caused her state of panic to escalate into outright terror.

"All right," she seethed. "But I'm not becoming any kind of surrogate mother—or unpaid teacher—just be-cause you're totally ignorant of kids, Riley Hanrahan, have you got that?"

For the first time since he'd read the letter, Riley looked full at her. In a hostile voice he said, "I wasn't aware I'd asked you to be either one."

Which put paid to that particular conversation.

Twenty-five minutes later Morgan turned off the high-way to a side street, following it up the steep slope of the mountain toward a huge brick house perched on the hillside. She pulled up in the semicircular driveway and turned off the engine. It was amazing, she thought, how much money must have been spent to produce so grace-less and ugly a dwelling. The brick was a drab gray, the design pretentious, and the grounds soullessly formal.

Morgan had always hated topiary. "Well," she said, "here we are."

"I may not know much about kids," Riley said, "but this joint looks more like a prison than a place for seven-year-olds."

The windows were blank. Like Bob Dinsey's eyes the day he'd pulled a knife in history class. "I don't like it," Morgan said, and shivered.

Riley shot her a quick glance. "Let's go," he said, and opened his door.

Until they'd arrived, Morgan had had every intention of sitting outside in the car. Now she knew nothing on earth would persuade her to let Riley go in there on his own. She also got out, glad she was wearing her new dress and boots. They walked through a row of yews carved into fat barrel shapes, and Riley rang the bell. The door looked like the door to a bank safe, thought Morgan.

The butler who opened the door had a face like a safe. An empty safe, she decided. Locked tight but nothing inside. Riley said formally, "Good morning."

"Good morning, sir."

"I'm Riley Hanrahan. I've come to see my daughter, Jennifer. Might I ask your name?"

The butler's face remained immobile. "Sneed, sir. This way, sir. I'll get Mr. Slater."

The brother who inherited the house, Morgan thought, as they were ushered into a living room with a wide view of the houses, highways and autumnal trees of the valley. The color scheme of the room was cream and the chesterfield set covered in the softest of leathers. Everything was expensive and Morgan craved not one object in the room. Riley was standing like a ramrod beside the gray brick fireplace which contained an immaculately tidy pile of logs.

"Mr. Hanrahan," a man's voice said heartily. "We

weren't expecting you to arrive unannounced. I'm Beth's brother, Lawrence Slater.'' He looked inquiringly at Morgan. ''I hadn't realized you were married.''

Lawrence. The name slammed through Morgan's chest as though it were a bullet. ''Lawrence'll pay us, and pay us good,'' Howard had said to Dez as she had crouched in the rabbitbrush near their truck. Now she saw Riley turn to face the other man, his whole body suddenly alert in the way a tiger is alert when it sights its prey; and knew she wouldn't want Riley for an enemy. ''I'm not married,'' Riley said smoothly. ''This is my friend Morgan Cassidy, Lawrence. You did say Lawrence, didn't you?''

Lawrence Slater said bluffly, ''I did, Riley, I did. After all, we're all in the same family now, aren't we? Might as well dispense with formality.''

Very deliberately Riley limped across the room to shake Lawrence's hand. Lawrence Slater was Morgan's height, his features with the pallor of the room, his hair and lashes an indeterminate shade of brown and his eyes light gray. He looked flabby, as though it were a long time since he'd actually walked up the hillside to his house.

Standing very close to him, Riley said affably, ''You should have hired killers with a few more clues, Lawrence. Because unfortunately they let your name drop in Miss Cassidy's hearing. Not smart, Lawrence, not smart at all. Of course it was lucky for me that Howard's such a bad shot and that Dez wasn't around when brains were handed out.''

Lawrence's pudgy fists were clenched at his sides. ''I have no idea what you're talking about.''

Riley continued as if Lawrence hadn't spoken. ''The other lucky thing was that Miss Cassidy came along and saved me from dying of blood loss and dehydration in the desert.'' He smiled, a smile that sent a frisson along

Morgan's spine. "I should have read Beth's will on the way over here. If I'd had an unfortunate accident—a fatal one this time—before meeting Jennifer, would the entire estate have reverted to you?"

Lawrence's cheeks flushed a dull, unhealthy red. "You can't march in here and make all these accusations," he blustered. "I'll call my lawyer. I'll sue you for slander."

"No, Lawrence, you've got it wrong," Riley said softly. "*I'll* be calling *my* lawyer, to make a new will. Let me tell you something else. Should anything happen to me, first there'll be a police inquiry, and second, Jenny will be raised by the order of nuns who raised me. They will, of course, inherit the money, as well." He gave the other man a wolfish smile. "I trust we understand each other."

A look of cunning flitted across Lawrence's face. "I'm sure you'd like to meet Jenny," he said, dredging up a smile. "Why don't I fetch her? I expect you'd like some time alone with her."

Riley gripped him by the sleeve. "Not yet, Lawrence. First Miss Cassidy is going to make a phone call. To Mr. Atherton, Beth's lawyer. Just to warn him that should there be any attempts on my life in the next few days—or hours—you're responsible." He flicked a glance at Morgan. "The phone's in the far corner of the room, Morgan."

Lawrence croaked, "I won't allow—"

"Shut up," said Riley.

Morgan, obediently, made her phone call. Wilfred Atherton did not, in her opinion, sound particularly surprised by her strange request. She added calmly, "I think Riley would appreciate it if you could come to our hotel room late this afternoon so he could draw up his own will...Five would be fine, thank you."

Riley grinned at her, a grin crackling with energy. "I

said the FBI should hire you,'' he said. Then he turned his attention back to Lawrence. Gripping him by the shirtfront, Riley said evenly, ''I don't want to lay eyes on you again. The butler will take me to Jenny and you can stay out of my way—just in case I forget I'm a civilized man who should depend on the law to redress wrongs. I didn't like being shot in the leg and left to die, Lawrence. I didn't like it at all.''

He loosed his hold. Lawrence, his eyes glazed, scuttled out of the room as though pursued by a whole phalanx of hit men. And Riley went to the archway and called for Sneed.

The butler said impassively, ''Sir?''

''I'd like you to take me to see Miss Jennifer, please.''

''This way, sir. Madam.''

Her heart thumping as though she'd run all the way up the slope to the house, Morgan followed the two men up the stairs.

CHAPTER NINE

THE staircase was marble, and there was a singularly hideous piece of modern art hanging in the big hallway; it rather reminded Morgan of an eviscerated chicken. Sneed led the way down a corridor, Morgan's heels clicking on the polished parquet. He tapped on the very last door. "Miss Jennifer? You have visitors."

The corridor was cool. All Morgan's nerves were on edge, while Riley looked like a man on his way to the scaffold. She wanted to tuck her arm in his, offer him comfort and support. But that, she thought bleakly, might give Jenny the wrong impression. That Morgan and Riley were a couple, and Morgan a potential new mother. She couldn't do that.

The door opened. Very politely Jenny Slater said, "How do you do?"

She was small and pale and fragile-looking, with long brown hair falling down her back; she was wearing a pink dress whose ruffled skirt had been ironed exquisitely. But it was her eyes that went straight to Morgan's heart, for they were Riley's eyes, an unquenchably deep blue. They were gazing somewhere in the vicinity of his knees.

For a moment Riley stood still, as though his shoes were glued to the gleaming oak floor. Then Jenny looked up at him, blue eyes meeting blue. Clumsily he hunkered down, bringing his face to her level. "How do you do, Jenny?" he said huskily. "I'm your father. Riley Hanrahan."

"You can come in if you like."

She had a gap between her front teeth. Aware with

125

some part of her brain of Sneed retreating down the corridor, Morgan stayed in the doorway. Jenny said, "This is my bedroom."

The room was very large and contained every conceivable toy to amuse a little girl. The bed and drapes had more pink ruffles, and the white-painted furniture had lots of gilt curlicues. There was a television set and VCR on the bureau. Quite suddenly Morgan wanted to cry.

Jenny was standing in the middle of the pink carpet, as though uncertain what to do now. Morgan was almost sure that had Jenny not thought it childish, she would have been sucking her thumb.

Riley stooped down again, favoring his leg. "Jenny," he said, "I'm really sorry about your mother. You must miss her a lot." Jenny nodded, fiddling with the ribbon around her waist.

"I want to tell you something," Riley went on. "I didn't know about you until today. I didn't know I was a father. Your father. If I'd known, I wouldn't have waited this long to come and meet you."

"Mummy said I didn't need a father."

Morgan watched a muscle jump in his jaw. Very carefully he said, "That was okay while you had your mother. But now we need each other. You need a father and I need a daughter." He smiled at her, a smile of such sweetness that Morgan's throat ached. "Will you show me some of your toys?"

"I packed my favorites," she said.

Riley blinked. "Packed them?"

Her eyes widened. "Aren't I coming with you? Sneed said I was and so did Mrs. Emerson."

"Yes, of course you are. But I hadn't expected you to be packed already."

"I've been packed for a whole week. It took you a long time to get here."

"I had an accident a few days ago," Riley said. "It left me with a sore leg, otherwise I'd have been here sooner. I'm sorry, Jenny."

"Is it getting better?" Jenny asked with old-fashioned punctiliousness.

"Much," Riley smiled. "Is that your suitcase?"

Jenny nodded. "I can't shut it, though. It's too full. Can you shut it?"

"Why don't you sit down on it while I zipper it shut, how's that? What have you got inside?"

"Some dresses and my teddy bear and my new winter coat and my boots with the fur on. And my favorite books and my crayons and my rock collection." She frowned. "Socks and underwear, too."

"Did you pack all by yourself?"

"Oh, yes. Mrs. Emerson wouldn't have let me take my rock collection and Sneed thinks children should be seen and not heard."

This last was obviously a direct quote. So Jenny was packed and ready to go, thought Morgan, and realized that at one level she was enraged with Beth Slater. Couldn't she have hired a butler who liked children, or a housekeeper who understood the importance of a rock collection? The other thing she'd noticed was that not once, so far, had Jenny mentioned her uncle's name.

Jenny plumped herself down on the suitcase. But she was too small to bring the edges of the zipper close enough together. Peering down at the arm of a teddy bear that was protruding from one side, she said, "You could ask her to sit beside me."

For a moment Riley looked at a loss. Then he glanced up and saw Morgan stationed by the door. He had forgotten about her, Morgan knew. Forgotten her completely. Given the circumstances, there was no reason for her to feel so horribly hurt.

"Morgan," Riley said awkwardly. "Of course...
Jenny, this is my friend, Morgan Cassidy."

Slowly Morgan walked into the room. "Hello,
Jenny," she said. "Will I break anything if I sit on the
suitcase?"

"I don't think so." As Morgan sat down on the lid,
Jenny said, "Your hair is awful red."

Riley stooped, struggling with the zipper. "It's like
maple leaves in autumn," he said.

"Mrs. Emerson uses red peppers a lot when she
cooks. That's what it's like," said Jenny. "Sort of an
explosion."

Riley smiled spontaneously at the comparison; and
Morgan sensed intuitively that this was a child who had
been thrust into her own imagination for company. A
very solitary child. Again she felt that upsurge of anger.

As Riley pulled the two edges of the suitcase together,
his head was within inches of Morgan's knee. She
wanted to touch him so badly that she had to clench her
fingers in her lap to stop herself. She said at random,
"Jenny, your hair is beautifully shiny."

"Mrs. Emerson rinses it with vinegar and squeezes
the water out so hard it hurts," Jenny said matter-of-
factly. "There. You did it. Now we can go."

Riley said soberly, "I'm staying in a hotel in the city
right now, Jenny, and we can't go to Maine straight
away because there are some legal matters that have to
be cleared up first. You're sure you want to leave here?
Because we won't be back. I'd arrange for a mover to
bring all your toys."

"I want to go," Jenny said, scuffing at the carpet with
the toe of her shiny patent leather shoe. She even had
ruffles on her socks, Morgan saw. "I don't like it here
without Mummy."

Riley's jaw tensed. "Okay. We'll get Sneed to put

your suitcase in the car, and you can say goodbye to
everyone.''

The goodbyes, as it turned out, were perfunctory. Mrs.
Emerson, as starched as Jenny was ruffled, did not offer
to hug the child. Sneed gave her the smallest of bows
and the most minimal of smiles. Riley said, ''We should
say goodbye to your uncle.''

For the first time there was real feeling in Jenny's
voice. ''I don't want to,'' she said. ''I don't like him.''

''In that case we'll go,'' Riley replied, and took his
daughter by the hand to lead her out into the sunshine.
Jenny didn't pull away. But she dropped Riley's hand
as soon as they got to the car.

Riley sat in the back with Jenny, while Morgan sat in
the front. Like a chauffeur, she thought, and drove away
from the gray brick house. She could see, in the rearview
mirror, tears slipping silently down Jenny's cheeks, and
watched as Riley passed her a tissue without offering
her facile words of comfort.

So far, she thought, for someone right out of his ele-
ment, Riley was being a wonderful father; and wondered
why that should make her feel so dismally unhappy.

At the hotel desk Riley booked the room adjoining
theirs. But when he unlocked their own door and ushered
Jenny in, she plunked herself down on the empty bed in
the room Morgan and Riley had been sharing and said
to Riley, ''Are you in the other bed?''

''Yes.''

''I'll sleep here, then.''

''There's another room through here,'' Riley said casually, opening the connecting door.

''I might be scared of the dark in there all by myself.
There's spiders under the bed, big hairy ones. They bite
you if you're bad, Mrs. Emerson said so.''

Morgan swallowed rage as big as a mountain and said,

just as casually as Riley, "That's okay, I'll sleep next door."

She busied herself moving her few belongings into the other room, and did her best to stifle the sensation of having been exiled. From paradise, she thought with poignant accuracy.

They then went for lunch in the hotel cafeteria. Jenny's manners were impeccable; but so far Morgan hadn't heard her laugh. After lunch Riley suggested a shopping expedition. "When you live with me in Maine, you'll wear jeans a lot," he said. "Maybe we should unpack your suitcase and see what you need."

"Mummy didn't like jeans."

"All the kids in school wear them, though."

Jenny's face lit up. "You mean I'll go to school? Real school?"

"On a yellow school bus," Riley said.

"Wow," said Jenny with a gap-toothed grin that gave her a gamine charm. As Riley smiled back, Morgan felt as though she were watching the first tendrils of love bind father and daughter together.

Then Jenny said, "Can your friend come shopping, too?"

Riley said noncommittally, "Would you like her to?"

"I never went shopping with Sneed or Uncle Lawrence."

What Jenny meant was that she'd never been shopping with a man before. Riley bent to undo the suitcase. "I'm sure Morgan will come with us, then."

Unpacking the suitcase meant that a photograph of Jenny's mother was put on the stand by Jenny's bed. Beth Slater hadn't been merely pretty, Morgan decided painfully. There was true beauty in the austere line of her jaw and the level gray eyes, and only a woman with excellent bone structure could have worn her hair in so severe a style. But it wasn't a face Morgan warmed to. It was a face practiced in keeping people at a distance.

Just as Riley had been keeping her at a distance ever since they'd gone to the big brick house.

The shopping expedition made several things clear to Morgan. Jenny, who had lived in luxurious surroundings, was touchingly grateful for the jeans and sweatshirts Riley bought her, and adored her new sneakers with the orange neon laces. Riley, for his part, seemed intent on relegating Morgan to as minor a role as possible, nor was he subtle about it. Occasionally he was forced to ask her opinion, and Jenny insisted Morgan go with her into the fitting rooms. But other than that, Morgan might as well have been one of the dressmaker's dummies that stood about in the store, blank-faced vehicles for holding up clothes.

Finally, of course, Morgan couldn't protest his tactics. Not in front of Jenny. Which didn't improve her temper.

At five sharp Mr. Atherton knocked on the door of their room. Jenny was wearing as many of her new clothes as she could get on at once. "Well," said Wilfred Atherton, "don't you look nice? I like your sneakers."

While he and Riley went into the other room to talk business, Morgan started to read to Jenny from one of the books that had made the suitcase so heavy. Before Morgan had even finished one chapter of *Winnie the Pooh*, Jenny's dark lashes, so like her father's, had drifted to her cheeks and she was asleep.

Morgan and she were lying on Jenny's bed, their heads propped up on the pillows. It seemed to be taking Riley and the lawyer a very long time, thought Morgan, liking the weight of Jenny's body in the curve of her arm, feeling enormous compassion for what she sensed was a monumental loneliness. At least, she was calling it compassion. She didn't want to label it tenderness.

That would be too dangerous. Because very soon Riley and Jenny would be going to Maine, just the two of them; and she, Morgan, would resume her camping expedition in the desert.

She didn't want to think about that. She closed her own eyes, and fell asleep as suddenly as if she'd been hit on the head.

She didn't hear Wilfred Atherton leave through the other door. She didn't see Riley stand as if poleaxed in the connecting doorway when he saw his daughter and Morgan asleep on the big bed, Jenny curled into Morgan as confidingly as a kitten to a mother cat. She did become aware of a weight on the bed beside her, of warm fingers stroking her hair back. Drowsily she opened her eyes and smiled at Riley. Still half asleep, she murmured, "I missed you."

His lips brushed hers with tantalizing sensuality. "Me, too," he said.

She went to reach for him and suddenly realized that her arm was trapped beneath Jenny's sleeping body. "I'd forgotten about her," she said blankly.

Reality rushed back. She and Riley weren't alone in the motel in Sorel. They were in Salt Lake City with Riley's daughter: a very different scenario. She flinched away from Riley's touch. "You mustn't," she said, "not in front of Jenny."

Shutters dropped over his eyes. Restlessly he got up from the bed. "My leg's getting better," he said. "Finally. And the legal stuff should be all straightened out on Monday morning."

"Good," Morgan said with a false smile. "After that you'll be able to leave for Maine."

"I still feel as though any minute I'm going to wake up," he said in a low voice. "As though none of this is real. Yet at the same time I know it's absolutely real and that I've got to do my level best to make Jenny happy.

She *has* to come first.'' Obliquely he added, ''I couldn't bear for her to grow up in an orphanage.''

Morgan bit her lip. ''She doesn't have to. She has you, instead.''

As he sat down hard on the side of the bed, Jenny stirred. Yawning, the little girl looked up at Morgan. ''You didn't finish the story,'' she whispered.

Morgan managed a creditable laugh and picked up the book. ''The Heffalump has just been joined by another Woozle,'' she said, ''and Piglet's getting very nervous.''

When she'd finished the chapter, they went to McDonald's for supper. ''Mummy liked fancy restaurants better,'' Jenny said. ''But I think it's neat here.''

Riley bit into his hamburger. ''Mr. Atherton's invited us all over for an early supper tomorrow—it's Hallowe'en. Then you and his two little girls can get dressed up and go out for trick or treat.'' He smiled at Morgan, a smile that didn't quite reach his eyes. ''He says his wife has a whole closetful of stuff you and I can dress up in, too.''

Morgan had always liked Hallowe'en, accepting the fact that her students would be on a sugar-high for several days afterward from all the candy they'd been given. ''Sounds like fun,'' she said nonchalantly.

''Do you think he has a pumpkin costume?'' Jenny asked. ''Cinderella's coach was a pumpkin.'' Then she looked straight at Riley. ''What am I s'pposed to call you anyway?''

Riley looked disconcerted. ''What do you want to call me?''

''I'm not allowed to call grownups by their first name.''

''Oh…well, why don't we make an exception to that rule for now? You can call me Riley, and when you get more used to having me around, maybe you'll call me Dad.''

"Okay," said Jenny, not calling him anything, and ate her chips one at a time, dipping them neatly into a little heap of ketchup.

Back at the hotel they watched a rerun of "Sesame Street." By the time Jenny was bathed, a ritual she insisted Morgan share, and Riley had read two more chapters of *Winnie the Pooh*, Morgan was exhausted. Riley turned the far lamp on as low as it would go. "We'll be in the next room, Jenny, but we won't shut the door." He hesitated. "Sleep well," he added gruffly, and kissed her on the forehead. "I'm very glad you're coming to live with me."

Jenny clutched her worn blue bear to her chest. "I hope they do have a pumpkin costume," she said, and scrunched her eyes shut. Five minutes later she was asleep.

In the adjoining room, which also had two beds, Riley sank down on the nearer one. "Fatherhood's a full-time occupation," he said in a dazed voice. "I don't even have a room set up for her at home. Do you think she'll be okay, Morgan?"

"It's bound to take her a while to get used to you. And she must be grieving for her mother."

"Yeah…one of the reasons I accepted Wilfred's invitation was so I could take him aside and pump him about Beth. Did you hate that house as much as I did?"

Cautiously, Morgan also sat down. She felt as though she'd been wearing her new dress forever and all she wanted to do was strip it off and make mad, passionate love to Riley. Who, handsome though he looked in his gray trousers and white shirt, would look very much more handsome without them. Good luck, she thought ironically, and said, "I hated the house, everything in it and all its inhabitants. Except Jenny, of course. How *could* that Mrs. Emerson have frightened her with tales about spiders?"

"How could Beth have hired her and why didn't Jenny go to school?" He rubbed at his forehead. "I had Wilfred draw up a letter for Lawrence that should, in its very dry legal way, put the fear of God in him...I've decided not to prosecute, by the way, for Jenny's sake. But while I'm on the subject of Lawrence, I owe you an apology, Morgan—it wasn't outside the bounds of possibility that Howard and Dez might have tried again here in the city." He looked over at her, making no attempt to touch her. "I'll pay for your parking ticket and the worst thing about all this is that we can't sleep together."

Morgan had come to that conclusion herself. It didn't help to have Riley tell her something she already knew. "Just as well, I suppose," she said. "Stops us from getting in too deep."

"How deep is too deep? Are you wearing your black bra?"

She stood up, jamming her hands in her pockets. "Stop it!"

He stood up, too, limping around the end of the bed until he was only a foot away from her. Morgan stood her ground, her heart pounding. He said with brutal honesty, "What if we're both in way over our heads? Then what do we do?" Leaning forward, he kissed her hard, a kiss that began in frustration and anger, but flared almost instantly to the passionate desire Morgan remembered so well.

She jerked her head back. In genuine anguish she cried, "Please, Riley, don't! We can't make love, Jenny might wake up. So don't torment me like this, I can't bear it."

He lifted his head, and briefly his eyes were calculating. "Seems to me you're in pretty deep, Morgan Cassidy."

Her nostrils flared. "Did you do that on purpose?"

"I sometimes feel I have to drag stuff out of you."

"It's sex," she hissed. "That's all that's between us. Sex."

His features hardened. "I don't think so."

"I know so." In a flurry of blue denim she pushed him away. "Do you know what's so awful about all this? We can't even have a decent fight!"

"And by the look of you, you're spoiling for one," he drawled. It wasn't until he flicked her chin with his finger that she realized how formidably angry he was. "I thought I was the only one who was out of my league when it came to intimacy. I'm beginning to think you've got just as much to learn as I have. If not more. Time's running out, Morgan. You might want to think about that when you sleep in here all by yourself. Do you always want to be by yourself? Is that what you want out of life? Or do you want to risk whatever the hell it is that intimacy means?"

As she gaped at him, too taken aback to muster a retort, he kissed her parted lips with angry emphasis and marched out of the room.

He left the door ajar.

Morgan thought dark thoughts about symbolism, scrubbed at her lips with the back of her hand and flung herself down on the bed. The other thing she couldn't do, besides make love with Riley or yell at him at the top of her lungs, was to sob her heart out.

Morgan woke in the middle of the night. She had been dreaming, a dream whose details had instantly fled but whose atmosphere of dread was still sitting like a dead weight on her chest. Something had wakened her.

Then she heard it, through the door that she had been too proud to shut: Jenny's little shriek of fear.

Morgan was out of bed in a flash, her silk gown swirling around her ankles. As she hurried to the door a band of light suddenly fell through it. Riley had switched on the bedside lamp.

She stopped in her tracks, holding her breath. Cautiously, keeping to the shadows, she peered through the door.

The first thing that struck her with a jolt of surprise was that Riley was wearing pajamas. Of course, she thought, that's what he bought earlier today when he asked me to watch Jenny for a few minutes in that department store. Now she watched his blue-clad back bend over Jenny's bed and heard him say softly, "Jenny, wake up, you're having a bad dream. It's okay, it's Riley…"

The little girl sat bolt upright, her eyes huge in her face. "The spiders, they're gonna get me!"

"It's a dream, sweetie," Riley said, taking her in his arms with an unpracticed gentleness that touched Morgan to the core. "You're safe here with me, I won't let them get you."

"I want my mummy," Jenny wailed, and collapsed into his chest in a storm of weeping.

Morgan drew back, feeling tears crowd her own eyes. She could hear Riley murmuring words of comfort, and knew exactly what she had to do.

Go back to bed. Leave the two of them alone. It's called, she thought with an unhappy twist of her mouth, building a relationship. And she was definitely not part of that process.

She knew something else. Riley was repairing old wounds. As a little boy he'd been left alone with his nightmares; Sister Anna hadn't been there to comfort him. Now, as a grown man, he was making sure Jenny wasn't alone.

She crept back to bed, drew the covers up to her chin and let tears slide silently down her cheeks. How could

she be jealous of a seven-year-old? That was a despi-
cable way to feel.

But it wasn't really jealousy. Jenny wasn't taking anything that was Morgan's. She was simply, by her presence, depriving Morgan of what she wanted. Riley's
arms around her. Now. In the dark. His big body alongside her in the bed, his hands teaching her the many and
joyous ways of lovemaking.

Of lovemaking, not love.

That was what the dream had been about, she realized.
Deprivation and loss. It had been grief sitting on her
chest as heavily as that ugly brick house sat on the hillside.

Hugging her arms around her body, she lay very still.
It was a long time before she fell asleep again, and when
Jenny's little voice piped from the door, ''Come on, it's
time to get up,'' Morgan felt as though she'd only just
closed her eyes.

''What's the time?'' she mumbled, untangling herself
from the covers and stretching her arms over her head.

''Breakfast time,'' Riley said.

Morgan's head jerked up. He was standing in the
doorway, fully dressed, looking both relaxed and well-
rested; there was a new ease to him, as though Jenny's
nightmare had indeed done more than assuage a dream
about spiders. Jenny, wearing her new jeans, was hop-
ping up and down. ''We're going to eat at a restaurant
that makes strawberry pancakes and I'm wearing my
sneakers with the orange laces,'' she crowed. ''Hurry
up!''

She didn't look like a little girl who had wept for her
mother in the middle of night. Jenny's tears, Morgan
thought gloomily, had obviously been cathartic. Which
was more than could be said for her own. ''Count me
out,'' she yawned. ''I'm going to sleep in.''

"No, you're not!" Jenny cried, running over to the bed. "I'm going to tickle you, that'll wake you up."

As Jenny bounced onto the bed, Morgan caught a gleam in Riley's eye that was all too familiar. "Go away—both of you!" she yelped.

Ineptly, but with great enthusiasm, Jenny started to tickle her. Morgan began to giggle, trying to hide under the covers. But Jenny yanked at them, and with a catch at her heart Morgan heard her laugh, a rich chortle full of delight. "All right," Morgan gasped, "I surrender. Give me ten minutes and I'll be ready."

"Eight minutes," said Riley.

The covers were down to Morgan's waist and the silk nightgown hadn't been designed with modesty in mind. She sat up, hitching at the straps and tossing back her tumbled, gleaming curls. Glaring at him, she repeated, "Ten minutes."

Like a man impelled by forces beyond his control, Riley bent and kissed her full on the mouth, the quick flick of his tongue like the dart of fire. Then he said calmly, as though nothing had happened, "Okay, Jen, let's go or she'll never be ready."

Jenny grabbed him by the hand and hauled him out of the room. This time Riley closed the door behind him. Morgan pulled a face at it, a face worthy of a Hallowe'en mask, and got out of bed. Exactly nine minutes later she was ready.

They ate breakfast in a pancake house; Morgan downed rather a lot of hot coffee. Then they drove to a park with a playground, where Jenny got mud on her new sneakers and had to be comforted by Riley. As he was wiping it off, Jenny said, "I'm not allowed to get dirty."

"Let's make an exception to that rule, too," Riley said easily. "When you're in your jeans and sneakers, you can get as dirty as you like."

Jenny looked at him doubtfully. "You're not like my mummy."

"I don't suppose I am."

Jenny looked down at Morgan's feet. "You've got dirt on your boots."

Morgan smiled. "When I go camping in the desert, I get very dirty. Sometimes it's fun to get dirty."

She could see Jenny struggling with this new concept. "Let's go on the swings," the little girl said. "Push me, Riley?"

It was the first time she'd called him by name. Morgan watched something in his face change, and wished herself a million miles away. Or even two hundred, she thought, wandering off to a bench under some trees. My campsite on the ledge would do just fine.

She wanted to weep again. She'd never had much time for women who cried a lot. That'll teach me to be more tolerant, she thought, and sat down on the bench. She knew exactly what was wrong. She felt as though she'd been given a wondrous gift, the gift of Riley's body and of her own passion, a passion she hadn't known existed until she'd made love with Riley. And now, before she could fully appreciate that gift, it had been snatched from her. By circumstances quite beyond her control and with nobody and nothing to blame but fate.

Jenny would be happy with Riley. And Riley with Jenny.

But Riley's fatherhood had certainly put paid to an affair so new that Morgan didn't know how to categorize it. Or how to deal with its termination, she thought miserably.

The shadows of the pine trees danced over the dirt, where the sun lay warm. In sudden defiance Morgan vowed to go down laughing. Not weeping. Tomorrow she'd head back to the desert, where she could cry all

she liked. But today was Hallowe'en, All Hallows' Eve.
A night to dance and laugh and have fun.

Afterward the desert would heal her. It always had.

She got up and strode over to the swings and pushed
herself off; and Jenny, certainly, couldn't have guessed
that Morgan had a care in the world.

CHAPTER TEN

THE Athertons lived in Layton, a suburb of Salt Lake City, in a pleasant bungalow that backed onto a wooded ravine. Wilfred met them at the door, showing Jenny the quail pecking in the grass behind their house, and telling her to watch for the deer who often helped themselves to the fallen apples under the trees. The house was flanked by an array of pumpkins with fearsomely carved faces, while a white-robed ghost hung from the ginkgo tree out front. Wilfred, out of his business suit, looked younger and more relaxed; his wife Pat was a charming blonde, a family doctor whose untidy house was very welcoming. Morgan felt instantly at home.

Their two girls, Lee and Sarah, were nine and seven respectively. They ignored Jenny's tendency to hang back; and soon all three were involved in a rowdy board game.

Supper, a rather haphazard affair, nevertheless tasted delicious. All four adults helped clean up afterward, then Pat said, "Want to come down to the basement, Jenny? Our cat had kittens four weeks ago."

"Come on, Jenny," Sarah cried. "They're real cute."

As Morgan also started for the basement door, Riley put an arm on her sleeve. "Stay here, Morgan," he said, "I want you to hear this, too."

It was the first time he'd touched Morgan since that early morning kiss. And if their affair was over, what was the point of her hearing anything more to do with Jenny? "I like kittens," she said stubbornly. "Let go."

Instead Riley held fast to her arm, hooked the basement door shut with his good leg and looked over at

Wilfred, who was putting away the last of the silverware. "Tell us about Beth, Wilfred, what she was like as a mother. I couldn't believe that house. Mrs. Emerson starched like a ramrod, and Sneed like a dessicated corpse in a suit of armor."

"You exaggerate," Morgan said in a staccato voice. "A corpse implies a live body. He was like a safe. Locked tight with nothing of value inside."

For a moment the old Riley was back, with his crooked smile that always made her knees weak. "Dead on, Morgan," he laughed, and hugged her spontaneously.

Her body responded to him like tall grass to the wind. Wilfred smiled benevolently. "I don't know that there's anything I can say about Beth that you haven't already figured out."

"Try me," said Riley inflexibly.

Playing with the clasp on the silver chest, Wilfred said with legal exactitude, "Beth wasn't a bad woman, or a cruel one. But I think she'd forgotten what it was like to be young. She treated Jenny more like a possession than a child. A possession to be polished and put on show occasionally. But not a possession to be shared— she never brought her here, for instance, to play with our girls."

"And hence no public schools."

"Exactly. Jenny's a bright little thing, and probably knows more from books than she'd have learned in school. But in other ways she's missed out, and I think one of the best things you can do for her is put her in a regular school. In," he smiled again, "regular clothes. You should have heard Pat on the subject of the ruffled dresses after the one time she met Beth and Jenny." With gentle malice he added, "Jenny, of course, went to the best pediatrician in town. No family practitioners for her."

"No sense of humor," Riley said. "Beth, that is."

"Absolutely none." Wilfred put the chest away. "Never marry a woman without a sense of humor. It'd be very boring."

"You can't be calm and serene and have a sense of humor," Morgan remarked to the ceiling.

"Touché," Riley said. "One more thing, Wilfred. As soon as the business end of things is cleared up, I plan to head for Maine with Jenny. Is that wise, do you think? Or should I wait around here until she gets more used to me?"

"Go," Wilfred said promptly. "She'll remember what she needs to, and the rest she won't miss."

"That's sort of what I thought," Riley said quietly, and for a moment rested his gaze on Morgan. Morgan looked back, giving nothing away. He put an arm around her waist and said, "Let's go check out the kittens."

Leave me alone, she wanted to scream. If this is part of the game called intimacy, you're cheating and I don't want to play.

The kittens were adorable. Rashly, Riley said, "When we get settled in Maine, maybe we could find you a cat or a kitten, Jenny." Jenny clasped her hands in delight, temporarily speechless. Morgan, once again, felt like weeping.

She was greatly relieved when Pat drew her into another room. "Are you and Riley going to dress up, Morgan? We do have a pumpkin costume for Jenny, and I've got a pirate's outfit that Riley, I have to say, would look absolutely devastating in." She added without a trace of envy, "Quite a man you've got yourself there."

"Humph," said Morgan. "Have you got a witch costume? A really ugly one. That's what I want to wear."

"As a matter of fact, I do." Pat hesitated, then said indirectly, "Motherhood can be extraordinarily fulfilling, you know, even if there are days when an oil rig in the middle of the ocean looks appealing. And now I'll mind my own business, Wilfred always says I involve myself far too much in other people's lives, but then as I say to him, legal jargon does the exact opposite, don't you agree?''

Morgan nodded weakly. Pat didn't have any problems with intimacy. Riley should find himself a woman like Pat. There were probably dozens of them back in Maine who'd be falling all over themselves to mother Jenny for him. And warm his bed.

She hated each and every one of them.

The witch costume was beginning to seem more and more appropriate. It consisted of a long black cloak, a peaked hat, a corncob broom and a quite ghastly mask through which Morgan's eyes glittered and around which her red hair flamed. "Maybe I'll scare Jenny," she said doubtfully. "I don't want to do that. She woke up last night with a bad dream."

"Kids are a lot tougher than you think. And this is Hallowe'en, you'll be fine."

Morgan left the basement room where she'd changed and went upstairs. Jenny was encased in a fat orange pumpkin, her arms sticking out and her legs in black stockings. An orange and green cap was anchored over her bunched-up hair. Pat said, "Hold still, Jenny, and I'll make up your face for you."

Lee was Big Bird and Sarah was practicing growling in her role as Oscar the Grouch. Wilfred made a surprisingly dashing highwayman, while Riley as a pirate took Morgan's breath away. Riley took one look at her and began to laugh. "Am I finally seeing your true self?"

"Just keep me away from any cauldrons."

He came closer and said for her ears alone, "I need a spell. I want it cast over a woman who's bewitchingly beautiful but exceedingly stubborn. Can you help me out?''

''I could break the bewitchment.''

''It would take a coven of witches to do that. How in heck can I kiss you with that mask on?''

''You can't,'' Morgan said, and wished his shoulders didn't look quite so broad in his full-sleeved shirt, which was open halfway down his chest. ''You'll catch pneumonia,'' she added fractiously.

''There's a cloak.'' He picked it up off the table and swirled it around his shoulders. ''I rather like this cloak. Perhaps I'm living in the wrong century.''

Pat had given him a black mustache and a patch over one eye, the combination making him look both rakish and dangerous. It was a good thing, thought Morgan, that they'd be chaperoned by Wilfred and three small children. A very good thing.

Five minutes later they set out, the children equipped with large plastic pumpkins to hold their treats. Darkness had already fallen, and the streets were busy with other children, dressed as goblins, Frankensteins, princesses and ghosts. Parents hovered in the background.

At first Jenny hung close to Riley. But after a few houses, when she'd been given chips, chocolate bars and a fudge stick, she pushed her way to the front at the next door, hollering, ''Trick or treat!'' in a very unladylike way.

Under different circumstances Morgan would have been enjoying herself. The costumes, the candlelit pumpkins and the ghoulishly decorated gardens were all great fun; and she loved watching Jenny enjoy herself. The trouble was, she loved it too much. Jenny, after all, was nothing to her. Jenny belonged to Riley.

When the children's pumpkins started to overflow with treats, Wilfred said, ''Time to head back, girls. You can give Mum a hand at the door handing out candy, how's that?''

"And we've got to sort out our loot," Sarah cried. "You got tons, too, Jenny."

Jenny gave a little skip of delight. "Let's go back and eat some."

"Wilfred," Riley said, "would you mind very much if Morgan and I hang back? There's something I want to talk to her about, and one of the things I've already learned about being a father is the absence of privacy."

Behind her mask Morgan made a muffled sound of protest. Both men ignored it. "No problem," Wilfred said amiably. "Take your time—they can always watch a Walt Disney video while they're stuffing their faces with junk."

"Thanks," Riley said, pushed up his eye patch and said to Jenny, "Morgan and I are going for a short walk, Jenny. You'll be okay with Wilfred and the girls?"

"And the kittens," said Jenny with a cherubic smile, and hurried after Lee and Sarah, clutching her candy to her fat orange chest.

Riley took Morgan by her black-cloaked arm. "Let's go," he said, and led her in the opposite direction to Wilfred's. She scuttled along beside him; her feet were hurting in her black boots and she was sweltering behind her mask. When they'd reached a quieter section of the street, Riley slowed down, pulled her mask away and kissed her very thoroughly. "You smell of rubber," he said, "and you taste like heaven."

She had not attempted to struggle. What was the use? And besides, this was sex. This was the one part of their relationship that she understood. When he released her, she said pithily, "You'd have made a good pirate. Take what you want and to the devil with the consequences."

"Morgan," Riley said, "while you were getting dressed in this rig, I phoned the airline. I made three bookings to Maine for tomorrow afternoon that I have to pay for tomorrow morning. Will you come with us?''

Her jaw dropped. "Me?" she squeaked.

"Yes," he said with monumental patience. "You."

"No," she said feebly. "Oh, no, I can't do that."

He took her by the shoulders. He was standing with his back to a house whose owners had strung scarecrows dressed in ragged clothes from the trees, and planted plastic gravestones under the trees; the figures waved back and forth in the breeze, the porch light casting shadows sharp-edged as knives. Morgan yanked her mask from around her neck and pulled off her witch's hat, wishing this was happening somewhere else to someone else.

Riley said, "You don't have to go back to school until after Christmas. You'd like where I live, right by the sea. Give us a chance, Morgan. Come with us tomorrow."

"Don't you hear what you're saying?" she said jaggedly. "Us, us, us. You've got Jenny, Riley. You don't need me."

"You've got that wrong. I do need you."

"As Jenny's surrogate mother?" she flashed.

"No! But Jenny exists, Morgan. She's my daughter and I have to do the very best I can for her. For now, she has to come first, don't you see that?"

"As you never came first in the orphanage," Morgan answered with unhappy truth.

He grimaced. "That's right. I have to give her all that I'm capable of. No matter what the cost is to me. To you and me."

"The timing's all wrong," Morgan said wildly. "It's too soon, Riley. Much too soon."

"Too soon for what?"

The wind was ruffling his hair and the scarecrows swayed in a horrible travesty of hanged men. "You and

I. That's what I mean. We met under circumstances that weren't exactly ordinary, and then four nights ago we started going to bed together and it's all new and I don't have a clue what's going on, and then all of a sudden you find out that you have a child. A seven-year-old daughter who needs you. I can't handle it, Riley. It's too much pressure.''

''I know the timing's atrocious, do you think I haven't figured that out? But it is what it is, Morgan, and that's what we've got to work with.'' He pushed her hair back from her face. ''I'm not asking you to move in with me. But you could rent a cottage near us, and we could see each other on a regular basis. Take our time.'' He gave her a faint smile. ''Go on dates, go to the movies, walk on the beach. Normal stuff. No gunshots or rattlesnakes. No melodrama.''

It was on the tip of Morgan's tongue to ask, ''Riley, do you love me?'' But she wasn't sure she wanted to hear the answer to that particular question. ''You're nothing like the kind of man I've always pictured myself getting involved with,'' she said with a kind of desperate honesty. ''All we do is fight and have incendiary sex. You can't build a relationship on that.''

''How do you know? Have you ever tried?''

''Why would I?'' she said shortly.

''You didn't fight with Chip or Tomas, and sex with them was a big yawn. Or so you said.''

''I want the kind of marriage my parents had,'' Morgan retorted, and wondered why she didn't sound more forceful. ''There's nothing wrong with steadiness and affection.''

''I never said there was. In fact, I could do with big doses of both, and so, I'm sure, could Jenny. But be careful here, Morgan. You know what I think you're looking for? Perfection. The perfect man. Who'll never raise his voice or upset you or make any demands on you that you don't want to fulfill, and who'll give you a nice, boring life in suburbia with 2.4 children.''

"I'm not!"

But Riley was warming to his theme. "That's what it is—you're looking for Mr. Perfection. Well, let me tell you something. He doesn't exist. He's a figment of your imagination. But I exist, Morgan. I'm real. Not perfect. I've got a temper, and I hate being helpless and dependent, and intimacy scares me to death. And I'd sure as hell make demands on you. Because—and you can now add arrogance to the list of my faults—I think you were only half alive until I came along. I watched your face the first time we made love. It was as though a part of you emerged that had never seen the light of day.''

For a moment Morgan was struck dumb. She had come to much the same conclusions herself, that Riley made her feel vibrantly, if not always comfortably, alive. "That was in bed," she said. "I'm not denying that sex with you was absolutely astounding."

"*Was*?" he repeated sharply.

"Jenny doesn't need a third person around. She needs to accept you as her father and grow to love you without someone else like me hovering around on the sidelines. Riley, I loathe this conversation, can't we go back to Wilfred's?"

"You've got far too much courage to run away like this!" With a sigh of frustration he dropped his arms to his sides. "Here's another of my faults—I hate begging. But Morgan, please come with us tomorrow. Please.''

"No," she said. "I couldn't possibly do that."

His back was to the light, his face in shadow. She had no idea what he was thinking. Or feeling. She herself felt raw all over, and once again she wanted to weep. A downpour like a desert rain. She jammed her mask back on her face and her hat on her head, and started back toward the Athertons' house. Riley, in silence, followed her.

The streets were emptying of children, she noticed vaguely. It must be getting late.

Too late. Too soon. Had she ever, even on the worst of days in school, been this tired?

The next couple of hours passed in a blur for Morgan. The three girls were engrossed in the adventures of the *Lion King*, each with a rationed heap of treats in front of them. Morgan got rid of her witch costume, had a drink, made conversation that apparently made sense, and ate rather a lot of nachos and salsa. Eventually she and Riley drove back to the hotel.

Jenny fell asleep in the car. Riley carried the little girl up to their room; the sight of Jenny's long brown hair falling over Riley's sleeve filled Morgan with a tumult of emotions, chief of which was pain. Dammit, she raged inwardly, this is ridiculous, I'm wallowing in sentiment.

At the adjoining doorway, as Riley bent to deposit Jenny on the bed, Morgan said coldly, "Good night."

"Good night," he responded, just as coldly. "Jenny, it's okay, I just want to get your pajamas on."

Morgan closed the door. She had a stomachache, she was as jittery as a canyon wren, and she knew she couldn't possibly go to bed yet. She went into the bathroom, replenished her makeup and brushed her hair, and left the room. First she went to the cafeteria, where she ate a club sandwich. Then she walked into the bar.

It was attractively laid out, with velvet-covered wing chairs grouped around small tables; in the far corner a pianist was playing jazz, rather well. Morgan ordered a vodka and orange and leaned back in her chair, listening to the notes wander over the keyboard without apparent purpose yet somehow achieving a coherent whole.

It was time to go back to the desert. First thing tomorrow that's what she'd do.

This decision made her feel minimally better. She ate some peanuts and slowly drank her vodka.

A dark-haired man walked into the bar and looked around.

He saw her almost immediately. He strode over to her table, sat down and signaled to the waiter. "Scotch on the rocks, and another drink for the lady," Riley said. Turning to Morgan, he added, "Jenny didn't even wake up. The hotel provides a baby-sitting service, but I shouldn't stay long in case she has another nightmare."

"I should have left the hotel," Morgan said shrewishly. "That way you wouldn't have found me."

"I'd have caught up with you sooner or later."

He tossed back some peanuts. Their drinks were delivered. Leaning forward, Riley said, "I wasn't thinking straight out there at Wilfred's. All that stuff about the flight tomorrow, I blew it. It hit me while I was putting Jenny to bed. What I really want."

He took a gulp of Scotch. "The timing's as bad as it can be and I won't make any fancy speeches about falling in love with you because I'm not sure I even know what that means. But I do know one thing. I can't bear for you to stay in Utah tomorrow while I fly right across the country with Jenny. Leaving you behind."

As she opened her mouth to protest, he said, "Just hear me out, will you?" and took another long drink. "I want you to marry me," he said, with as much emotion in his voice, thought Morgan, as if they were discussing the purchase of another pair of boots. "I was an idiot to say I didn't want you to move in. Of course I do, but as my wife, and if I insulted you with all that talk about rented cottages, I'm truly sorry. I'm also very thankful I worked this out before I got on the plane tomorrow."

He smiled at her, clearly relieved to have his speech over with, and drained his drink.

Distantly Morgan was aware of gratitude that he'd

phrased his proposal so ineptly; because that way it was easy for her to refuse. Sitting up straight, she said, ''You didn't insult me with the rented cottage. But you sure have insulted me by asking me to marry you when you don't even love me. And in case you're wondering, the answer's no.'' She added belatedly, ''Thank you.''

''I didn't say I don't love you! I said I didn't know what love is.''

''Then I suggest you find out before you propose to anyone else.''

''Morgan,'' he rasped, ''I figure I've waited thirty-five years for you to come along. I'm not about to ask anyone else to marry me.''

''Then why, ever since Jenny's appeared on the scene, have you behaved as though I'm an inconvenient stage prop? Something to be tripped over or shoved out of the way.''

''I didn't know how to treat you! I want to make love to you so badly it must be written all over me—but it's not a message for Jenny to read. Plus I don't have a clue what the future holds for you and me. I can't afford to raise false expectations in her mind, now can I? Making Jenny trust me is my number one priority, surely even you can see that?''

''The only thing I can see,'' Morgan said stonily, ''is that our affair is over. Over before it really began. Quite frankly, I wish it had never—''

''Can I get you another drink, sir?''

Morgan gave a nervous start; she hadn't noticed the waiter. ''Yes,'' said Riley, ''a double,'' and passed him a couple of bills. Then he said forcefully, ''I don't want our affair, as you call it, to be over. I've never been in love with a woman before, so I don't know what it's like. I don't know the lingo. But I'll tell you how I feel about you. You thrill me the same way I'm thrilled when a great blue whale rises from the waves, its spume blowing like mist in the wind. You're as joyous as dolphins at play, as dangerous as a hurricane at sea, as indecipherable to me as whale song echoing in the deep. To think of losing you hurts me in the same deep place that I hurt when I have to watch a beached whale dying in the sand.''

Struck dumb, Morgan gazed at him. Never in her life had anyone spoken to her that way. She felt humbled and inadequate and achingly sad. Because, of course, she didn't love Riley.

''That's the only language I know, Morgan. Not the language of romance and red roses.'' He gave a sudden, wry grin. ''I don't even like red roses.''

The waiter deposited the glass of Scotch on the table. Leaving the drink untouched, Riley said urgently, ''Marry me, Morgan. It'll work out, I know it in my bones. Because I think we met for a reason, out there in the desert. We were meant to meet.'' He smiled again, that lopsided smile that always made her melt inside. ''Maybe we owe Lawrence a vote of thanks.''

Morgan gulped the last of her drink and didn't smile back. She felt as though the day had gone on for far too long. Wishing she could conjure up some anger, hating herself for saying what she was about to say but knowing she had no choice, she muttered, ''It's a beautiful language, Riley, and more than I deserve.'' Bravely she looked straight at him. ''I can't marry you because I don't love you. It's that simple.'' As though she had to repeat herself in order to know her words for the truth, she said, ''I'm not in love with you. In like and in lust, maybe. But not in love. I'm *sorry*. And now I need to go upstairs because I'm pretty sure I'm going to cry like a bucket. Don't come up with me—please?''

She got to her feet, clutching her wallet. Riley stood up, too. He looked very pale in the dim light. ''So this really is goodbye.''

"I'm not going to check out of the hotel tonight because I'll have to say goodbye to Jenny in the morning," she babbled. "So I'll see you tomorrow. Good night, Riley."

She ran across the carpet, took the first elevator to their floor and unlocked her door. Then she locked the adjoining door, fell across the bed and smothered her sobs in the pillows.

The next morning remained for a long time in Morgan's memory as the worst in her life. She showered, realizing it would be her last one for a while, dressed in her bush pants and dark green shirt and braided her hair. She also threw all her new clothes into their boxes and bags. When Jenny tapped on her door, she was packed. "Hello, Jenny," she said brightly. "Ready for breakfast?"

The three of them ate in the hotel cafeteria. Riley was putting on a good act for Jenny's sake, but Morgan could recognize all too clearly the marks on his face of a sleepless night. She herself looked very much like a woman who had cried herself to sleep. Ten showers couldn't have changed that.

They went back upstairs. Once they were in the room, Riley said, "Morgan has to leave soon, Jenny. She's not coming with us to Maine."

Jenny had been reaching for her bear. She stopped and looked around at Morgan. "You're coming on the plane with us," she said confidently.

"No, Jenny," Morgan said, her throat dry. "I'm staying here. I'm going camping in the desert."

"But I want you to come with us!"

"I can't."

Jenny's little mouth drooped, her eyes the same stubborn blue as her father's. "I want you to come on the plane, too," she repeated obstinately. "I like you."

Almost, Morgan changed her mind. Almost. "Riley will take very good care of you and you'll love your new school," she said weakly. "But I'm on vacation still, and that's why I'm going camping." She kissed Jenny on the cheek and wasn't surprised when the little girl pulled away. "I'd better get going, I've got a long drive ahead of me."

Riley handed her an envelope. "My address and phone number. I live in a little place called Machin's Cove in northern Maine. I want your address in Boston."

"I probably won't be back there for quite a while."

"Morgan."

She flinched at his tone, scribbled the information on a piece of the hotel stationery and said breathlessly, "Goodbye, Riley. I hope you and Jenny have a good flight."

He made no attempt to kiss her. His face was locked against her. Like Sneed's, she thought numbly, and fled next door to gather up her gear. Fifteen minutes later she'd checked out and was driving away from the hotel.

Away from a man who had brought her body to life, and from a child who in two short days had found a place in her heart.

Morgan put her foot on the accelerator and headed for the interstate.

CHAPTER ELEVEN

MORGAN camped for a week on the ledge in the desert.

For the first three days she tried very hard not to think about Riley. She hiked each day until her body was exhausted, read assiduously in the evenings, cooked her meals and slept poorly; although she could censor her thoughts in the daytime, she couldn't control her dreams. And nearly all of them were about Riley.

Some were almost pornographic in their explicitness, waking her to a rage of desire for a man she had repudiated. Others were more threatening. Storms at sea, where Riley was washed overboard and no one would come to his aid. Herself entangled in sheafs of fishnet, drowning while Riley swam past her uncaring of her plight. Worst of all were the plane crashes, because those involved Jenny as well as Riley.

The desert, which had always furnished her with peace, was failing her. She felt the very opposite of peaceful. She felt as though she were being slowly and agonizingly torn apart.

But why? After all, she'd been the one to leave Riley. If he'd had his way, she'd be in Maine right now.

Married to a man who didn't love her?

Yet what of herself? She'd told Riley she didn't love him; and she'd meant it. But now that she'd regained her precious solitude, she was haunted by him, obsessed by him; and everywhere she went, a dull ache of discord and loss went with her.

Solitude had become loneliness, and the loneliness was unbearable.

By the fourth day Morgan knew she had to do some-

157

thing. She hiked to the highway and drove into Sorel, where she phoned Mike Prescott's business number. "He's between patients," the receptionist said with the air of one conferring an enormous if unwarranted favor. "Hold for a minute."

"Prescott here."

"Mike, it's Morgan Cassidy...you met me with Riley."

"Morgan, of course. Is Riley with you?"

"No, he's gone back to Maine. I don't suppose you're free for lunch?"

"Half an hour from now in the salad bar on Anasazi Avenue."

Keeping to his word, he was there right on time. "Great to see you again," he said with a big smile. "When did Riley leave?"

Morgan, clutching the menu to her chest, burst into tears.

Horrified at herself, she saw Mike fish out a clean handkerchief, pass it to her, and order two spinach salads, all with the efficiency of one used to much more drastic emergencies. She blew her nose hard. "I don't know what's wrong with me," she snuffled. "He asked me to marry him."

"Good God!" said Mike.

"And he hates red roses," she wailed.

Mike looked at her quizzically. "I suppose they're your favorite flower."

"I hate them, too. And we both knew Sneed was as hollow as—as a pumpkin on Hallowe'en." Her face crumpled again; she scrubbed at her cheeks so vigorously they were as red as any rose. "Plus he's got a seven-year-old daughter called Jenny."

"A *daughter*?"

Understandably Mike looked befuddled. "That's why the lawyer wanted to see him in Salt Lake City,"

Morgan explained. "They went to Maine together four days ago."

Recovering fast, Mike said with gentle irony, "Riley and the lawyer?"

"Very funny," she snorted. "Her name's Jenny."

"So you bolted," Mike said.

Her head snapped up. "I did not," she replied in an unfriendly voice.

"Ran away, then. Tail between your legs. What's the matter, Morgan? Don't like kids?"

"I like them very much," she said with as much dignity as she could muster when she had a red nose and red-rimmed eyes.

"You and Riley—bad sex?"

The red in her cheeks deepened. "No. Fantastic and utterly wonderful sex."

"So why aren't you packing up your tent and heading for Maine? It's obvious the guy's head over heels in love with you."

"It might be obvious to you. It isn't to him. Or me."

"He must be. Riley has never come anywhere near asking a woman to marry him."

She clipped off the words one by one. "He has not once told me that he loves me."

"Sometimes actions speak louder than words. Riley Hanrahan proposing marriage is one such action, trust me." Mike chewed on a piece of bread. "Interesting, though. I always suspected that Riley would meet the right woman one day, and fall in love. And do you know why I thought that? Because of the whales. He loves them. I've seen him struggle for hours to rescue a beached whale, and I've heard some of his speeches against the resumption of the whaling fleets. He cares about those creatures so strongly that it's kept love alive inside him all these years. Am I making any sense?"

"You're saying he's always had the capacity to love

and that's how he's exercised it,'' she said thoughtfully. ''With animals rather than people.''

''Right.'' Mike frowned at her. ''Do you love him, though? Because if you don't, this whole conversation is pointless.''

''I just don't know!'' Fresh tears welled in her eyes. ''I didn't think so. I told him I wasn't. But look at me, I'm a wreck. I've cried enough in the last few days to make peach trees bloom in the desert.''

''I've long believed the opposite to love isn't hate. It's indifference,'' Mike said. ''You don't exactly look indifferent to Riley, Morgan.''

The waitress deposited two heaped spinach salads in front of them, along with a basket of crisp French bread. Morgan, to her surprise, found she was hungry. For a few minutes they ate in silence. Then Mike said, ''Let me tell you something. Once when Riley and I were in New York City for a class reunion, he took me to the orphanage where he grew up. One of the sisters had died, a Sister Anna, and they were having a memorial mass for her.''

''She was the one he loved.''

''He told you that, did he? In the short time we were there I could see that the nuns were kind, doing the very best they could. But the buildings were institutional to a degree. Cheap paint, dormitories like barracks, a dining hall in which the temperature hovered around fifty-five degrees—it was February. And no privacy. I could see why Riley would turn into himself in that environment, and become a loner. He lived there for sixteen years, after all. And he never knew his parents. So if he has difficulty knowing if he loves you, or putting that into words, there's a reason.''

With a sharp pang Morgan remembered the words Riley had used, words whose beauty and poignancy had touched her heart. They were private words, she thought, not to be shared with Mike. "You're right, I know," she said. "And something else has just clicked for me. Riley never had a father, and yet he's had fatherhood thrust upon him. From what I saw, he was doing his best and his best was admirable…Trouble is, he kept turning me off in the process. Acting as if I was Mother Superior one minute, asking me to marry him the next. And," she finished with a sniffle, "we couldn't even sleep together. It was awful."

In an uncanny echo of Riley's words Mike remarked, "I never said he was perfect. Just human. Like the rest of us."

"My parents had a perfect marriage."

Mike gave a rude snort. "Ain't no such animal."

Her temper rose. "So *you* say! My parents were always there and always the same. Not a bit like Riley. I never know where I am with him."

Mike stared her down. "I'd take Riley Hanrahan's word to the bank any day of the week. If he says he'll be there for you, he's there. So maybe it's time you paid your parents a visit. Looked at them with new eyes."

"Oh." Morgan's heartbeat quickened. "They live in Maine," she said in a small voice.

"Even better," Mike rejoined. "Eat your lunch, Morgan."

They talked for another three-quarters of an hour before Mike glanced at his watch and threw a twenty-dollar bill on the table. "First appointment in ten minutes. Cynthia—my receptionist—has me terrorized, so I don't dare be late." He kissed Morgan on the cheek. "Send me an invitation to the wedding."

"You're an optimist," she said. But there was laughter lurking in her green eyes.

"Too right. Life's short and true love isn't as common as one might think. Take care, Morgan."

"Thanks, Mike," she said with obvious sincerity.

"I'd do a lot more than this for Riley. He's one of the best." He hurried outdoors, a thin, vital man whom she liked very much. You could learn a great deal about someone from his friends, she decided. Riley had a very good friend in Mike.

Morgan didn't pack up her tent when she went back to the ledge. Not right away. Subconsciously, perhaps, she wanted to give Riley and Jenny more time together. But also she wanted time to think about Riley and herself, to remember all that they had done together; to remember her own past, as well.

If Riley had never been in love before, neither had she. Not really in love. So she had nothing with which to compare her feelings. Had she been fooling herself for years to think she wanted a marriage just like her parents'? As peaceful and placid as a village pond?

Riley wasn't a village pond. Riley was like the ocean he loved. Tumultuous, never still, full of undercurrents and hidden depths. And beauty, she thought, gazing at the orange glory of the setting sun on her seventh evening in the desert. In giving her the best gifts of his body and soul, he had opened her to the beauty that can unite a man and a woman.

The desert that had nourished her for years was a lot more like the ocean than it was like a village pond. Could it be that Riley was truly her mate, calling to her body in the most primitive way possible, yet also matching her soul?

The next morning Morgan packed her gear, drove into Sorel, phoned her parents, and booked a flight out of Salt Lake City. She also phoned Mike to tell him she was going to Maine. "My parents live near Portland, I'm going there first." With a momentous sense that her whole future lay in the balance she added, "But probably I'll drive north to Riley's place after that. I guess."

"Go for it," said Mike, "I'll be rooting for you. Tell

him I want to be best man. Gotta go, Morgan, Cynthia's giving me the eye.'' And he rang off.

Morgan got in her car and drove to Salt Lake City, where she took her car back to the rental agency. The next morning she flew to Portland. Her father met her at the airport, and her mother was standing on the front step when the car turned into their driveway. Their house was a charming saltbox painted antique blue with gray trim; honeysuckle vines and roses twined around the windows. Some of the roses were still in bloom. Frances, her mother, looked after the flowers in the front garden, while Harold Cassidy managed the vegetable plot in the back. I feel like I'm stepping into a magazine article, Morgan thought, climbing out of the car. The perfect house and garden, which shelter the perfect marriage. Her mother was still a very pretty woman, with her graying curls and rosy cheeks; her father, as he aged, looked more and more distinguished.

Her heart was beating very fast. She kissed her mother and they went inside.

Dinner was perfect, too. Cornish game hens with wild rice stuffing, squash and beans from the garden, and a delectable pumpkin pie. They chatted about unimportant matters throughout the meal. But as Frances poured the coffee, Harold said, "You look more rested, Morgan. I've never understood how camping in one of the most inhospitable ecosystems in the country can do that for you, but it works every time."

In a rush, before she could lose her courage, Morgan said, "I met a man. While I was out there. Can I ask you both something?"

"Of course, darling. I do hope he's nice," said Frances.

"Nice isn't quite how I'd describe him."

"He's good to you, I trust," her father said sternly,

polishing his new bifocals on one of the immaculate handkerchiefs that his wife ironed for him every week.

Morgan didn't want to talk about Riley. Not yet. She said desperately, "All my life I've thought I wanted a marriage just like yours. That's why I stayed so long with Chip, because he was so easygoing and we never argued about anything. The two of you've been married for nearly thirty-three years, and I lived with you for eighteen of those years. I don't ever recall hearing you argue."

Frances looked at Harold, who looked back at her. Both of them seemed at a loss for words. Morgan blundered on. "Didn't you ever fight? In all those years?"

"Not fight," said Harold.

"We'd disagree sometimes," Frances said.

"Have differences of opinion."

"Even argue. But not fight."

Morgan's head had swiveled back and forth throughout this interchange. "But I never heard you!" she said urgently. "Not once."

"That's because we never argued when you were around," Frances said primly.

"When your mother was first pregnant," Harold said with a fond glance at Frances, "we agreed we'd never raise our voices in front of you."

"And we stuck to it."

"So you did fight," Morgan said in a dazed voice.

"I do wish you wouldn't use that word," Frances said with unaccustomed sharpness.

"Riley and I—Riley's his name—we fight all the time," Morgan said forcibly. "Yell at each other. Challenge each other. And often," her mouth softened, "end up laughing at each other. It makes me feel alive, Mum. Fight's the right word for it. The only word. For me, at least."

"It's a word I can't stand," Frances announced, flustered and pink-cheeked.

"Why?" Morgan asked bluntly.

"Really, Morgan," Harold interposed, "this is scarcely appropriate conversation for the dinner table."

"I flew all the way from Salt Lake City to have this conversation," Morgan said, her gaze holding her father's without backing down. "It's very important to me."

Harold looked at Frances, who looked back, and it was as though a wordless communication passed between them. Morgan had seen this happen before; it was one of the reasons she had so often thought her parents had a perfect marriage. Frances said, "Harold, I'd like a liqueur. A Cointreau, please. Morgan, will you join me?"

"I'll have a Tia Maria, Dad, please." She fiddled with her coffee spoon until Harold had put the three small glasses on the table; Frances very rarely indulged in alcohol.

Frances raised her glass and drank. Her cheeks grew a little pinker. "I've never told you this before, Morgan," she said. "But you're twenty-nine, I have to realize that you're not a baby anymore. And I'd dearly love to see you married and settled with a nice man."

Her mother had never before mentioned that Morgan's unmarried state wasn't to her liking. "Riley is a very fine man," Morgan said quietly, knowing her words for the truth.

"He'd have to be in order to be good enough for you," Frances said. "I never really did like Chip, Morgan. A bit wishy-washy, if you don't mind me saying so."

"I don't mind," Morgan said. "Riley isn't wishy-washy."

"Good." Frances took another decorous sip of

Cointreau and said rapidly, "My parents—your grand-parents, although you wouldn't remember them, they died before you were two—they fought all the time. Shouting, throwing things, arguing incessantly about anything from what to have for dinner to where they wanted to be buried. I hated it. I absolutely hated it."

To her dismay Morgan saw that her mother's eyes were glittering with tears. "Mum..." she said, and reached over to pat her hand.

Frances gripped her daughter's fingers very tightly. "Nowadays they probably would have divorced. But in those days it wasn't that easy." With a dignity that sat well on her, she went on, "From the time I was old enough to think about marriage, I vowed I'd never fight in front of my children. Ever. If my husband and I had issues over which we couldn't agree, we'd sort them out behind closed doors."

She patted at her eyes with her napkin. "Harold supported me in that, and that's how we brought you up." A tear trembled on her lashes. "Did we do wrong, Morgan?"

Harold made a small gesture with one hand. Morgan said strongly, "Of course not. You gave me a wonderful childhood, which is the very best gift parents can give. It's only now that I've met Riley that I needed to know more."

"Don't marry him if you're going to fight all the time!"

"It's not mean or dirty fighting, Mum. There's not a mean bone in that man's body." She screwed up her face in thought. "It's as though we strike sparks off each other. He's been a loner all his life, and I suppose, despite the fact that I've taught school all these years, I am, too. So we're a bit like two stray cats, circling each other, not sure if we can trust each other, testing each other out."

"How does he earn his living?" Harold said. "You'd better tell us more about him."

"I will. In a minute. But there's something else I want to ask." Morgan paused. "It's about sex," she said. "I—you're not a demonstrative couple and I've wondered…"

"Really, Morgan," said Frances, whose ancestors had been New England Puritans.

Harold said nothing. Instead he got up from the table, walked to the other end, drew Frances to her feet and kissed her. With undoubted passion for a man of fifty-nine after thirty-three years of marriage.

"There," he said, smiling down at his wife, "does that answer your question, Morgan?"

Frances said, "Sex belongs behind closed doors, too." She looked rather like a hen with ruffled feathers. But not an unhappy hen, thought Morgan. Rather a smug hen, in fact.

"Thanks, Dad. I believe it does," Morgan said meekly.

Harold strolled back to his chair. "Good," he said.

His blue eyes were gleaming. He reminded her of Riley right after he'd scored a point in one of their arguments, Morgan realized with a catch in her heart. Maybe she hadn't been so far off base to want a marriage like the one her parents had shared for so long. Because what she'd learned in the past few minutes was that it wasn't a perfect marriage so much as a real one. Enlivened by disagreements, yet infused with a love and passion that had flourished for years.

Harold said calmly, "I want the man's name, age and occupation. For starters."

Morgan obliged, and soon discovered that she loved talking about Riley to two people who were interested because they loved her. She edited her sexual exploits, and finished by telling them about Jenny. Frances said dubiously, "That's an awfully big responsibility."

"I'd like to take it on, though," Morgan said. "If he'll still have me. He never really said he loved me, you see. And I did hightail it back to the desert in sort of a hurry." She blanched. "Maybe he's met someone else."

"In a week? If he has, then you don't want anything to do with him," Frances said, very fiercely for Frances. "You must bring him up to meet us, darling. And Jenny, as well, of course."

"I watched a program on whales just the other day," Harold said. "It would be most interesting to talk to an expert."

So Riley and Jenny would both be welcome in the house in which she, Morgan, had grown up. A lump in her throat, Morgan said, "Thanks. Just wish me luck, will you? The thought of actually going to his house scares me to death."

Frances said, "Nonsense. If he's half the man you say he is, he'll be waiting for you with bated breath and open arms. Why don't you phone him, darling?"

"I couldn't," Morgan gasped. "I've just got to turn up on his doorstep. When I see his face, then I'll know."

"Would you move there?" Harold asked. "What about your job?"

During her last four days in the desert Morgan had given her job some concentrated thought. "I need a change," she said. "I've done a long enough stint in an inner-city school for now, and burnout's no fun. I'd like to try some of the lower grades in a more rural area. So I'm going to hand in my resignation in Boston no matter what happens. I'll have to get relicensed, too."

"Makes sense," Harold said. "I've worried about you the last year or so."

"Not half as much as I have," Frances interjected. "And it would be lovely to have you closer, dear." She smiled at her husband. "Morgan can borrow my car to go to Riley's house. We won't need both cars for the next few days, will we, Harold?"

"Not at all," said Harold, and raised his glass in a toast. "Good luck, Morgan."

The next morning Morgan and her mother went shopping. This was a delaying tactic on Morgan's part, because she didn't want to arrive in Machin's Cove until after Jenny had gone to bed. It was going to be difficult enough facing Riley, without adding the complication of Jenny.

Frances Cassidy loved to shop. Before she knew it, Morgan had been persuaded to buy a gored skirt in fine black wool and a dramatic black sweater decorated with swirls of green and tangerine that looked quite marvelous with her hair and eyes.

She said to her mother, "This is the third time I've bought clothes to give myself courage—I'd better sort out this romance fast, or I'll be in the poorhouse."

"That sweater is perfect with your boots and raincoat," Frances said with a pleased smile. "You can't turn up at the man's front door in those dreadful bush pants."

"Any more that I could go to the desert in this," Morgan teased, swirling the skirt around her knees.

As matter-of-factly as if she were discussing the price of the skirt, Frances added, "You know you're in love with him."

"I know nothing of the kind," Morgan said warmly. "That's one of the things I haven't figured out yet."

"Darling, I watched your face last night while you were talking about him. I've never seen you look remotely like that before. Of course you're in love with him."

"Oh," said Morgan, and took out her credit card. Her

mother, she knew from years of experience, could be remarkably intuitive on occasion.

After lunch she loaded all her gear in Frances's car, kissed her parents goodbye and drove away with the image of them standing together on the front step, their arms around each other. In thirty years' time, might she and Riley be doing the same thing?

Don't think about Riley. Not yet.

She meandered north, taking her time, visiting secondhand bookstores along the way. She had dinner in Ellsworth, the nearest place of any size to Machin's Cove; she only had another twenty miles or so of driving. After she'd eaten, she went to the washroom to clean her teeth. This outfit's all wrong, she thought, panic-stricken. I don't want Riley to see me all dressed up. I want to look the way I looked the first time we met.

Morgan hurried outside. It had started to rain. She rummaged through her pack until she found her bush pants, her green shirt and her hiking boots, changed in the washroom and pulled her hair back with a ribbon.

That's better, she thought. Now I look real. Not perfect.

She bundled her new clothes into a plastic bag in the back seat in a way Frances would have deplored. Then she set off again. It was dark, the highway slick with rain, nor was she sure of the way. In Cranberry Head she stopped at a gas station and asked for directions. "You can't miss the turnoff," the attendant said cheerfully.

She did miss it, and had to backtrack. But eventually a small sign reading "Machin's Cove" caught her headlights. A general store was still open amidst a cluster of houses. She went inside and asked how to find Riley Hanrahan's house.

"He's the whale feller, right? Go another mile or so,

and you'll see a long driveway off to your right—his place is right on the sea. It's a blue mailbox unless I'm misrememberin'. Yeah, I'm sure it's blue.''

''Thanks,'' Morgan said, and ran outside into the rain.

The blue mailbox was unmistakable and had Riley's name inscribed on it in neat black lettering. Morgan pulled off the road and turned off the motor. She was going to walk up the driveway. Despite all her stops, it was still only seven o'clock, and Jenny probably wasn't in bed yet.

As she climbed out of the car and locked it, a new sound came to her ears: the steady roar of breakers. The sea was very close, the sea that was Riley's first love. Morgan zipped up her rain jacket, pocketed her keys and waited until she had her night vision. Then she walked up the dirt driveway as though she knew exactly where she was going and why.

Neither of which was true.

CHAPTER TWELVE

As MORGAN walked along the driveway, the mingled scents of decaying leaves and wet evergreens were sharpened by the ocean's salt tang. I'm entering Riley's territory now, she thought. As different from the desert as it could be, yet just as wild and uncontrollable.

The driveway wound between the trees until through the branches she caught the first gleam of light. She slowed, approaching more cautiously, keeping her body in darkness as she got closer and closer to the house; and all the while she was aware of a keen curiosity to see where he lived.

Even with its back toward her, it was a beautiful house, built of stained cedar with tall granite chimneys and wooden shakes on the roof. As she edged through the wet, dense firs, she was relieved that she had followed her instincts and dressed in her hiking gear. This was no place for her new leather boots and shiny black raincoat.

The front of the house came into view. Tall windows, shaped like the prow of a ship, were angled toward the sea; Morgan could see spray rearing from the rocks, and to her ears came the thud and hiss of this age-old collision. She tucked herself well back in the trees, pushed back her hood and looked into Riley's living room.

With a lurch of her heart she saw that he was sitting on the chesterfield by a huge granite fireplace, where flames flickered and danced. Jenny was snuggled into him. He was reading to her. A very large black cat was curled in a ball on a cushion beside them.

Terror caught at Morgan's throat. They looked so contented, all three of them, so self-sufficient. A week ago Jenny wouldn't have cuddled that closely to her father; she wouldn't even hold his hand in Salt Lake City.

They didn't need her. They were doing fine without her.

And Riley had returned to the ocean that he loved, was surrounded by its dangers and its thrills. Even less would he need her, Morgan.

With a tiny whimper of distress Morgan sank down to the moss below the trees. A bough dumped a shower of water down her neck. She scarcely noticed it. She'd been an idiot to come here.

Riley finished the story and closed the book. Jenny threw herself at him and he stood up, swinging her over his head as she shrieked with delight. Then he walked out of the room, carrying her. He wasn't limping, Morgan thought dully. Even that was gone.

A ridge of bark was digging into her back. Her trousers were clinging to her legs, and raindrops trickled down her cheeks like tears. But for once, she thought with a gallant attempt at humor, she wasn't crying.

Riley was gone for over ten minutes, time that seemed to last forever to the woman crouched under the wet firs. She wished passionately that she'd never told her parents she was coming here. For it had been a fool's errand, one she should never have undertaken. She would have given everything she owned to find herself transposed to the ledge in the desert; if it could no longer bring her peace, at least it offered familiarity.

Her heart gave another of those disconcerting lurches in her rib cage as Riley came back in the room. He added a log to the fire, patted the cat, then went out again, reappearing a little later with a coffee mug in one hand and a newspaper in the other. He sat down and started to read.

Go back to your car, an insidious voice whispered in Morgan's ear. He'll never know you were here. He doesn't need you. Look at him. He has a beautiful house and a daughter who loves him. He's forgotten you already.

Morgan pushed herself up from the rock. She was only risking rejection and humiliation by staying here and confronting him. She didn't need either one.

Leave, Morgan. Now.

Morgan slithered back into the trees until she could no longer see Riley. Then she scrambled through the undergrowth, emerging partway along the driveway. It was raining harder; her jacket, supposedly waterproof, wasn't living up to its claim. She sloshed through a puddle. Her whole body felt numb and all her emotions seemed to have shut down. When she reached the highway, she stood by the door of her mother's car and fumbled in her pocket for the keys.

The vehicle came from nowhere, traveling fast, its headlights slicing through the darkness and the rain. Transfixed by the brilliant twin beams, Morgan thought for one frightful moment that it was going to hit her. Then it swerved, its horn blaring, and careened around the corner out of sight.

With a tiny moan of relief Morgan leaned against the car. She could have been killed…too close a call altogether.

But it had left her with her brain racing, her numbness gone; all her confusion had crystallized into clarity. She was running away again. Bolting, as Mike had called it. He'd been right. She had *run* away in Salt Lake City.

She wasn't going to run away again.

Morgan stumbled over to the shoulder of the road. Even though she was terrified of finding out that Riley didn't love her, she had to know. Once and for all. If he didn't love her, she'd leave right away and get a job in New Mexico. Or Texas. Somewhere as far from Maine as possible.

But first she had to know the truth.

For the second time that evening she worked her way through the drenched trees to the front of the house, where she stationed herself under a tall pine, absently brushing away the drops that had fallen on her face and hair. She'd wait fifteen minutes until she was sure Jenny was asleep and then she'd knock on Riley's door.

If he sends me away, at least I'll know he doesn't love me. And then maybe I'll be able to forget him.

Maybe.

Morgan shuddered, a shudder that had nothing to do with the damp and the cold. Shoving her hands in her pockets in a futile effort to warm them, she waited, the second hand on her watch creeping around the dial with agonizing slowness.

As though she were watching a movie, she saw Riley toss the paper down on the floor and get to his feet. He began pacing up and down, staring out into the darkness through the rain-streaked windows. She shrank back. He reminded her of an animal in a cage, one whose only choice was to accept boundaries that dealt a terrible violence to its whole nature. Chewing on her lip, she watched him go to stand by the fireplace, where he stared into the flames, his arm angled along the mantel, his hand banging rhythmically on its burnished wood.

With a suddenness that struck her like a blow, he dropped his forehead to the mantel, his shoulders in a despairing slump.

He looked defeated. Beaten. A man driven beyond his endurance, yet knowing that all he could do was endure.

Morgan's heart was thumping louder than the waves. She pushed herself upright and knew just what she had to do. Forgetting caution, she flung herself through the trees, lunging over roots and rocks, her one aim to reach Riley and, if it were humanly possible, to remove that corrosive despair.

Riley must have caught movement from the corner of his eye. His head swung around and he started for the door. Not watching where she was going, Morgan tripped over a rotting stump and fell to her knees. The sharp point of a dead bough scratched her cheek. With a yelp of pain she pressed her palm to the wound and kept going.

The light over the back door suddenly flooded through the trees, temporarily blinding her. ''Who's there?'' Riley shouted.

She staggered out of the trees and onto the driveway, looked at her hand and saw that it was covered with blood. What a good thing I didn't wear my new sweater, she thought, and in a wave of dizziness said, ''It's me.''

''*Morgan*!''

He looked as though he'd been hit on the head with a granite boulder. Did that mean he loved her? Or did it mean he didn't want her here? Why had she been so sure that seeing his face would tell her all she needed to know? Morgan took four more steps toward him. ''I—I came to see you,'' she said.

Top marks for intelligence, Morgan. You could tell him that it's raining, next. That would be another brilliant statement.

''What happened to your face?'' he said sharply. ''You're bleeding.''

''It's only blood,'' she said faintly. ''At least there's no melodrama.''

''I'd say it qualifies as melodrama,'' he said grimly. ''Darkness and rain and a woman I thought I'd never see again skulking through the trees around my house like a common thief.''

This was worse than anything she'd expected. Temporarily speechless, Morgan tried to staunch the wound on her cheek, succeeding only in spreading blood to her chin, her nose and her fingers.

The desert, she thought giddily. Why didn't I stay in the desert?

Riley started down the steps towards her. He was

wearing a dark blue sweater over faded jeans, and he moved with a loose-limbed grace that was new to her, used as she was to his limp. She stood rooted to the driveway, like a tree, and watched him reach out for her shoulder. She said frantically, warding him off, "Don't touch me!"

He flinched as though she'd struck him with a whip, and stopped in his tracks. Raindrops were already glittering in his thick, dark hair. She added desperately, "Not yet. That's what I mean. I've got to talk to you first."

He was looking at her as inimically as Howard had looked at her in the tamarisks. "At least let's talk inside," he said. "Or is it part of your plan that we have to stand here in the rain and catch pneumonia?"

"I know I'm doing a lousy job, Riley," Morgan gulped. "I'm sorry." She looked down at herself and added with faint surprise, "I am kind of wet, aren't I?"

"I've seen more than one drowned rat, and there's a strong resemblance."

His deep voice shivered along her nerves. She had always loved his voice, even when it sounded as downright hostile as it did now. She walked past him and climbed the stairs, entering a generously sized porch where a little yellow rain slicker that must belong to Jenny hung alongside Riley's much bigger one. "Is Jenny asleep?" Morgan asked.

"Yes. She drops off in an instant. A trait I've wished more than once in the last week that I could emulate. Here, give me your jacket."

He didn't sound at all welcoming. She passed it to him and bent to undo her boots. But her fingers were too cold to undo the knots. With an indecipherable exclamation Riley knelt at her feet and unlaced them. I won't cry, Morgan vowed, gazing down at his broad shoulders and bent head. I will not.

Not yet, anyway.

"Thanks," she muttered, and shucked them off. Her socks were wet, too, and her sodden trousers were like a second, clammy skin.

Riley said flatly, "You'd better come through to the bathroom and have a shower. Have you eaten?"

She nodded. "In Ellsworth. Coffee would be good, though."

He led her through a spacious kitchen and down the hall to the bathroom. It was paneled in cedar that scented the air; the floor was dark blue tile and the towels a matching dark blue. He said, "There's a robe on the back of the door."

She couldn't possibly say whatever it was she'd come here to say if she was half naked. Holding out her keys, she muttered, "My car's at the end of the driveway, and my clothes are inside. But be careful—a few minutes ago I nearly got sideswiped by someone speeding."

"More melodrama?" he said nastily. "You thrive on it, Morgan. I'll leave your stuff outside in the hall here." He then shut the bathroom door very firmly in her face.

He wasn't behaving like a man madly in love, thought Morgan. But neither was he indifferent; she'd stake her new black sweater on that. Turning away from the door, she scowled at her reflection in the mirror.

She looked like an escapee from a vampire movie. Blood and rain had mingled over most of her face, and her hair clung in a rusted tangle to her scalp. The blood made her feel sick to her stomach. Or perhaps it was tension that was doing that.

She stripped and stepped under a spray of the hottest water she could bear, then scrubbed herself dry. When she opened the bathroom door, her backpack and the array of plastic bags which contained all her new purchases were neatly lined up along the wall. Riley was nowhere to be seen. She found what she needed in her pack and grabbed the nearest bags. A few minutes later, her hair in a damp cloud around her face, a small plaster over the cut in her cheek and rather a lot of makeup on the rest of her face, she was ready. Chin in the air, she walked into the living room, a slim figure in a long gored skirt, black stockings, and a wildly patterned sweater that made her eyes look very green.

Riley stood up and passed her a mug of coffee. Morgan looked at it as though she'd never seen coffee before and put it down on a low pine table. The cat was now lying on the hearth. Digging her toes into the thick carpet, she looked up at Riley, the warmth of the fire caressing her ankles. "I don't have a clue what I'm going to say even though I've driven all this way to say it," she gasped. "But I know one thing. I did run away from you back in Salt Lake City. Because I was afraid." She ran her palms down the sides of her skirt. "I almost ran away again tonight. After I saw you and Jenny through the window, looking so happy."

His big body was very still. She had no idea what he was thinking. Now that she was close to him, she could see the marks of the last week in his face, marks that were surely those of exhaustion and unhappiness.

Taking heart from this, she blurted, "I went to see Mike last week. We talked about you a lot, and he told me more stuff about the orphanage and the whales. Then I went to see my parents and in one ten-minute conversation found out more about their marriage than I'd found out in twenty-nine years. It's a real marriage, not a perfect marriage, and I do want one like it." In a rush she added, "Mike thinks you're in love with me. My mother thinks I'm in love with you."

Riley's face hadn't changed. She said spiritedly, "Right now you sure don't look like a man in love. You look like you wish I was standing plunk in the path of a flash flood. I was a fool to come here. But I needed to hear you say you weren't in love with me. That you don't need me. That way I can disappear from your life and maybe I'll stop thinking about you all the time."

She hadn't intended to say any of this. Defiantly she finished, "I do need that coffee after all."

Clasping the mug gave her something to do; her fingers were still ice-cold. Riley said evenly, "And what do you think, Morgan? Do you think you're in love with me?"

A log snapped in the fireplace. The cat stretched and yawned; it was missing the tips of both ears and its blunt face was crisscrossed with scars. "That's not a very pretty cat," Morgan said.

"Jenny picked him out at the pound. He lost his ears to frostbite when he was a stray last winter. Don't change the subject."

It somehow seemed very typical of Riley that he go to the pound for a pet, and allow his daughter to pick out what must have been the homeliest animal there. Quite suddenly Morgan understood why she had flown across the continent and driven the length of a lonely peninsula through the rain of a November evening. "It's so simple," she said in a cracked voice. "Why I came here, I mean. It's been staring me in the face for days, but I couldn't see it."

Drawing on every bit of her courage, she put down the mug on the coffee table, stepped closer to Riley and cupped his face in her cold hands. "I don't just think I'm in love with you," she said. "I know I am. Of course I am. I was just the last one to figure it out." Before he could reply, she stood on her tiptoes and kissed him on the mouth, her lips moving with generous insistence over his, and knew she had never in her life done anything that was more real.

Then she moved back, waiting for his response. Would he push her away? Tell her she had indeed come on a fool's errand? Or would he welcome her into his life?

Her heart seemed to have climbed right up into her throat. As for Riley, he looked utterly blank, just as he'd looked on the back step when she'd appeared out of the darkness.

He said, in a voice she'd never heard him use before, "Oh, God, Morgan." Then she felt his arms go around her, felt him pull her to the length of his body as he kissed her with a fierce and all-consuming intimacy that enveloped her like fire, and felt, too, the thrust of his arousal. Oh, yes, she thought, oh yes, and dug her fingers into his hair, pressing the softness of her breasts into his chest.

With a wordless exclamation Riley swung her into his arms and carried her down the hallway to a door that he kicked open with one foot. Like a woman in a dream Morgan saw bookshelves and more tall windows overlooking the cove and a wide bed covered with a spread the dense green of the forest.

As he fell on top of her on the bed, she lifted his sweater, remembering through her fingertips the roughness of his body hair and the heat of his skin. She said, marveling at how easy it had all been, "I've come home, Riley."

"You are my home," he said, and kissed her with a hunger that removed any trace of shyness Morgan might have felt. So it was she who took his hand and guided it to her breast.

Smiling into his eyes, she said, "I couldn't find my black bra in all those plastic bags and I was too nervous to waste time looking."

His face convulsed as he felt the firm rise of her flesh. "You're so brave and so beautiful," he muttered, kissed her again and pulled his own sweater over his head. As he tugged at his jeans, Morgan fell across him, inhaling the scent of his skin that was so much the essence of the man and that she would remember, she was sure, until the day she died. Then he was naked to her. Naked and ready, this man whom she loved.

The rain pelted against the glass. She said quietly, "I

can see you and I can see the ocean behind you. We *are* alike, Riley, you and I, we both need our wild places.''

''You're my wild place as well as my home,'' he said roughly. ''Undress for me, Morgan. Now.''

With seductive grace she stood up by the bed, letting her skirt drop to the floor, drawing her sweater up over her nude breasts, then stripping off her long black stockings and wisp of black underwear. Riley buried his face in her belly, then slid lower, seeking out all her sensitivities until she arched like a taut bow and cried out to the arrow's long flight from her body.

He drew her down on the bed, gazing into her drowned eyes; with infinite patience he began caressing her until again she was whimpering with need. Then it was she who took the initiative, straddling him and sinking down onto him, watching the blue of his eyes darken to the black of night, hearing him gasp her name and his need of the release only she could bring him.

He lifted her by the hips and rolled over, covering her, thrusting into her, again and again; and she matched him, stroke for stroke, desire and love so entwined in every cell of her body that they were inseparable. As I am from Riley, thought Morgan, and knew that this, for her, was brand new.

Then thought was abandoned for feeling, a tumult of feeling like a storm at sea, as unstoppable as a flash flood. Her cries and his were joined, seabird to bird of the desert, cries that rose and fell and then were silent.

Morgan was trembling all over. She clung to Riley and when she could speak whispered, ''Love makes all the difference. Knowing I love you. It was as though I'd never made love before.''

He lifted himself on one elbow, and the hand he used to push her hair back from her face wasn't quite steady. He said huskily, ''I think it's time you asked a question, Morgan. Of me.''

''You mean whether you're in love with me?'' She

traced the hard angle of his cheekbone and played gently with his hair. "I don't even think I need to ask it."

"Ask me, Morgan."

"Riley," she said softly, "do you love me?"

"I love you, Morgan. With all my heart I love you."

There was a sheen of tears in his eyes. In quick distress she said, "Doesn't that make you happy?"

"So happy I haven't got words to describe it."

She drew his head down to her breast, holding him with all her strength; eventually he looked up, his breath wafting her cheek. "Do you know what? You're the only woman I've ever said those words to. Three small words. I love you. So simple and so terribly complex. I'm glad I've never said them to anyone else, Morgan, that they're yours alone. As I am. If you want me."

"Oh, yes," she said, her lips curving in the darkness, "I want you."

"Will you marry me?"

"Yes."

He lifted himself on his elbows, one on either side of her body. "That's it? A one-word yes? After all the grief I've been through the last week?"

"Dearest and most adorable Riley, I love you from the tips of my toes, which I have to say are a lot warmer now than they were fifteen minutes ago, to the top of my very messy hairdo. The thought of marrying you makes me so happy I might just levitate right off the bed."

"You're not going anywhere," Riley growled, and pressed her down into the mattress.

She wriggled her hips provocatively under his. "My mother comes from Puritan stock. I'm glad she can't see me now. Although the fact that you've proposed will endear you to her."

"That's good," Riley said. "You'd better lie still. Or you know what'll happen?"

She gave a delicate yawn. "More boring old sex?"

"Watch it," he said, "or we'll be having our first post-proposal fight."

With sudden intensity Morgan said, "Will Jenny be okay with us getting married? Maybe we should wait for a while, give her time to get used to the idea."

"She took to you from the start, Morgan, and all week she's kept bringing up your name. Which, I might as well tell you, didn't help me one iota. Why don't we have a Christmas wedding? That way I'll never forget our anniversary."

Morgan tickled him vengefully, Riley rained kisses on her throat and face, and quite a while later Riley said abruptly, "But what about your job, Morgan? Don't you have to go back to Boston to teach?"

"I'm going to send in my resignation," she said, and told him how she'd been thinking about a rural school. "It means I'll have to get a new licence, but I'm due for a change."

"You're sure?"

"Very sure. It had begun affecting my health, and there's not much point in that."

He kissed her again. "This week a contract I'd been negotiating with a publishing house in New York was finalized. I'm going to stay put the next year or so, look after the administration of the research station, and write a book about the whales, illustrated with my own photos. That'll give Jenny the chance to settle down without me having to go away at all." He gave her his lopsided smile. "You will move in, Morgan? Until Christmas. Despite your mother's Puritan ancestors?"

"I can't imagine being anywhere else."

He gave a sudden, incredulous laugh. "Pinch me. Just to make sure I'm not dreaming. I never want to go through another week like last week—although it taught me a thing or two. That I'm in love with you. That I'm incomplete without you. That intimacy's got something to do with wholeness."

Morgan said fervently, "That sounds like a lot."

"I'll tell you something else. I've already written one letter to your Boston address and left a very impassioned message on your answering machine. When Jenny and I got here and I realized how empty the house was without you, I decided I'd given up entirely too easily."

"I wasn't very encouraging."

"No, you weren't. But it had all happened too fast, it's no wonder we were both knocked sideways." Playing with a strand of her fiery hair, he added, "Thank you for turning up on my doorstep...I'll never forget you did that. For me. For us."

"You're very welcome," she said, snuggling into his chest.

He ran his hand along the tilt of her pelvis. "So do you think we're beginning to get the hang of this intimacy game?"

Her face lit with love, Morgan said, "I do believe we are. Although I'm sure there's always more to learn." She let her hand wander down his belly with deliberate sensuality.

"Then perhaps," said Riley, "we shouldn't waste any time. Because we'll have to behave ourselves when Jenny's around."

"I like misbehaving with you, Riley Hanrahan," Morgan said, and set out to show him just how much.

EPILOGUE

THE mechanical bleeps of an alarm clock woke Morgan. As her eyes flipped open, she discovered she was wrapped around Riley as tightly as ribbon around a parcel. Not that he seemed to mind. She said, smiling at him, "Does that noise mean we have to get up?"

He reached over and pushed a button on the clock radio, then nuzzled his lips into her neck. "Yeah. Or at least, I do. Jenny catches the school bus at eight-fifteen, and I usually shower before she wakes up."

"Why don't you do that while I start breakfast? That way I'll surprise her."

"Don't be in such an all-fired hurry," Riley growled. "You can kiss me first."

Kissing Riley meant that when Morgan next glanced at the clock, twelve minutes had passed. Passed very pleasurably indeed. She said, rubbing her nose against his chest, "You're not going to have time for a shower."

"We'll have to set the alarm half an hour earlier on school days," he said, kissing her again. "Right now, telling you I love you seems a whole lot more important than being clean."

"You really do love me?"

"Unarguably. Also lasciviously."

Morgan gave a breathless giggle as his hands showed her just what he meant. "I love you, too. Stop it! Or she'll never get to school."

He gave her one final kiss, then swung his legs out of bed. "Jenny likes the cereal in the blue box, with bananas chopped up on it, raisins stirred in, and lots of milk. The cat will try and tell you he's starving to death—don't believe a word of it.''

As Riley pulled on a dark blue robe and headed for the door, Morgan said, a catch in her voice, ''I do love you, Riley. I still can't quite believe I'm here. With you.''

He turned, his lopsided smile very much in evidence. ''Dearest Morgan...I've never in my life been so happy as I am right this minute.''

All her emotions coalescing into sheer joy, she wavered, ''You'll have to find some comic operas for the shower. None of this *Carmen* stuff.''

Laughing, he left the room. Morgan reluctantly untangled herself from the bedclothes, dressed in her black skirt and patterned sweater, and tried not very successfully to tame her hair in the small bathroom down the hall. Then she went into the kitchen and began opening cupboards and drawers, the black cat winding himself around her calves and doing his best to trip her. There was only one small niggling doubt in her mind: that Jenny might not be as excited to see her as she was to see Jenny.

The shower shut off, and a few minutes later Morgan heard Riley's deep voice mingling with Jenny's higher-pitched tones. The coffee was made and she'd put colorful red and blue place mats on the kitchen table. The cat, in a manner worthy of a baritone, was magnifying the level of his complaints; the tips of his ears might be missing, but there was nothing wrong with his voice. Fearing for the safety of her ankles, Morgan was about to search for cat food when footsteps ran down the hall and Jenny cried, ''Blackie, what a lot of—oh! *Morgan...*''

Morgan's nails were digging into her palms. ''Hello, Jenny,'' she said unevenly. ''It's lovely to see you again.''

Her eyes huge, Jenny said, ''Are you staying? For the

whole day? Will you still be here when I get home from school?''

Riley came up behind her. ''She's going to stay forever, Jenny. We're going to get married at Christmas.''

Jenny looked from Morgan to Riley and back, her face dazzled. Then she launched herself at Morgan, clinging to her with all her strength. ''Really? Truly? Forever?''

Morgan hugged her back, laughing and crying all at the same time. ''That's right. Is it okay with you?''

''Oh, yes,'' said Jenny. Then she gave Riley a reproachful look. ''Why didn't you tell me she was coming?''

''I didn't know,'' Riley said. ''It was a surprise.''

''A surprise to both of us,'' Morgan said, smiling at Riley with her heart in her eyes.

''For all three of us and Blackie, too,'' Jenny crowed. ''Isn't Blackie beautiful, Morgan?''

''Very,'' Morgan said; she had long believed there were times when the truth required stretching.

''He eats a lot. He keeps the nasty old spiders away in the night cause Dad lets him sleep on my bed.''

''Where else would he sleep?'' said Morgan.

''C'n I stay home from school today, Dad? Since Morgan's here?''

''No,'' Riley said firmly. ''She'll be here when you get home. And on the weekend perhaps we'll take a drive to meet her parents. You're going to inherit grandparents, Jenny.''

''Neat!'' Jenny said, and dumped dry cat food into Blackie's bowl. Blackie shoved his blunt nose into the bowl, shook a mouthful of pellets to make sure they were dead and started to purr. Jenny grabbed her bowl of cereal and sat down at the table. Nonstop she told Morgan all about the grade she was in, the new friends she'd made and the school play that would be presented next month. ''You could come with Dad,'' she finished.

''It's a date,'' Riley said promptly.

Jenny shoveled some cereal into her mouth. "Mary-lee's going to lend me some comic books, so I mustn't be late. Will you make my lunch, Dad?"

"Sure," Riley said, pouring the coffee and passing a mug to Morgan.

It was a small and very natural gesture. We're like a family, Morgan thought, the three of us around the table, the cat eating his breakfast. She said unsteadily, "I'm so happy I could burst."

"Me, too," Jenny said with her gap-toothed grin. "I like it here with Dad a lot, and you coming makes it abs'lutely perfect, Morgan."

"I second that," her father said.

Ten minutes later Jenny hugged Riley and Morgan and kissed Blackie's battle-scarred forehead before flying out of the door to catch the bus. Waving goodbye from the top step, his other arm around Morgan's shoulders, Riley said, "Can you believe it's the same child we saw waiting for us in the bedroom of that awful house?" Tugging gently on one of her curls, his smile very tender, he added, "Do you think that sometime she'd like a sister or a brother? A redhead?"

Morgan's lips curved. "I suspect she would."

"Once we're married, we'll have to see what we can do about that. In the meantime I'm going to phone the research station and say I won't be in today. Unless you have any objections?"

"I hope you didn't bother making the bed?"

"I decided it would be a waste of time," Riley replied, closed the door and took Morgan in his arms.

The bed was made at twenty to four that afternoon, five minutes before the school bus dropped Jenny off at the end of the driveway.

MILLS & BOON®

Next Month's Romances

♡

Each month you can choose from a wide variety of romance novels from Mills & Boon. Below are the new titles to look out for next month from the Presents™ and Enchanted™ series.

Presents™

THE DIAMOND BRIDE	Carole Mortimer
THE SHEIKH'S SEDUCTION	Emma Darcy
THE SEDUCTION PROJECT	Miranda Lee
THE UNMARRIED HUSBAND	Cathy Williams
THE TEMPTATION GAME	Kate Walker
THE GROOM'S DAUGHTER	Natalie Fox
HIS PERFECT WIFE	Susanne McCarthy
A FORBIDDEN MARRIAGE	Margaret Mayo

Enchanted™

BABY IN A MILLION	Rebecca Winters
MAKE BELIEVE ENGAGEMENT	Day Leclaire
THE WEDDING PROMISE	Grace Green
A MARRIAGE WORTH KEEPING	Kate Denton
TRIAL ENGAGEMENT	Barbara McMahon
ALMOST A FATHER	Pamela Bauer & Judy Kaye
MARRIED BY MISTAKE!	Renee Roszel
THE TENDERFOOT	Patricia Knoll

H1 9802

Available from WH Smith, John Menzies, Martins, Tesco and Asda

One special occasion—that changes your life for ever!

Everyone has special occasions in their life. Maybe an engagement, a wedding, an anniversary...or perhaps the birth of a baby.

We're therefore delighted to bring you this special new miniseries about times of celebration and excitement.

Starting in March 1998 in Enchanted™ we then alternate each month between the Presents™ and Enchanted series.

Look out initially for:

BABY IN A MILLION
by Rebecca Winters in March '98 (Enchanted)

RUNAWAY FIANCÉE
by Sally Wentworth in April '98 (Presents)

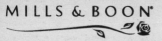
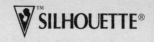